THE SHADOW-CAGE
and Other Tales of the Supernatural

There is nothing special about the little green stoppered bottle Ned Challis finds when he is out ploughing on Whistlers' Hill. It is chipped and dirty. Still, he takes it home with him, and the next day his daughter Lisa lends it to her cousin for a few hours. But Kevin leaves it in the school playground, and it is late that night, when he decides to go back for it, that he finds out how Whistlers' Hill got its name.

Quite ordinary things turn out to be haunted in the world Philippa Pearce creates – a funny little statue, an old biscuit-barrel, a nursery cupboard – and in quite ordinary circumstances. Memories of past unhappiness can cling to a place connected with them. Human passions can even reach beyond the grave if they're powerful enough: a mother longing for her daughter's return to the home which a cantankerous father has closed to her, an old man desperate at the neglect of his once-cherished garden.

Gently chilling, often poignant, these ten stories are written with all the fine perceptiveness and imagination for which their author is celebrated.

Philippa Pearce was born and brought up on the upper reaches of the River Cam, and the local countryside features in several of her books. She went to Girton College, Cambridge, and later worked as a scriptwriter and producer for the BBC and then in publishing. She won the Carnegie Medal for *Tom's Midnight Garden*.

Other books by Philippa Pearce

THE BATTLE OF BUBBLE AND SQUEAK
A DOG SO SMALL
THE ELM STREET LOT
LION AT SCHOOL AND OTHER STORIES
MINNOW ON THE SAY
TOM'S MIDNIGHT GARDEN
THE WAY TO SATTIN SHORE
WHAT THE NEIGHBOURS DID

The Shadow-Cage

and Other Tales of the Supernatural

Illustrated by
Chris Molan

PUFFIN BOOKS

Puffin Books, Penguin Books Ltd, Harmondsworth, Middlesex, England
Viking Penguin Inc., 40 West 23rd Street, New York, New York 10010, U.S.A.
Penguin Books Australia Ltd, Ringwood, Victoria, Australia
Penguin Books Canada Limited, 2801 John Street, Markham, Ontario, Canada L3R 1B4
Penguin Books (N.Z.) Ltd, 182–190 Wairau Road, Auckland 10, New Zealand

First published by Kestrel Books 1977
Published in Puffin Books 1978
Reprinted 1979, 1980, 1982, 1983, 1985, 1987

Made and printed in Great Britain by
Richard Clay Ltd, Bungay, Suffolk

Set in Monophoto Ehrhardt

*For Sally
in particular*

Contents

The Shadow-Cage

THE little green stoppered bottle had been waiting in the earth a long time for someone to find it. Ned Challis found it. High on his tractor as he ploughed the field, he'd been keeping a look-out, as usual, for whatever might turn up. Several times there had been worked flints; once, one of an enormous size.

Now sunlight glimmering on glass caught his eye. He stopped the tractor, climbed down, picked the bottle from the earth. He could tell at once that it wasn't all that old. Not as old as the flints that he'd taken to the museum in Castleford. Not as old as a coin he had once found, with the head of a Roman emperor on it. Not very old; but old.

Perhaps just useless old . . .

He held the bottle in the palm of his hand and thought of throwing it away. The lip of it was chipped badly, and the stopper of cork or wood had sunk into the neck. With his fingernail he tried to move it. The stopper had hardened into stone, and stuck there. Probably no one would ever get it out now without breaking the bottle. But then, why should anyone want to unstopper the bottle? It was empty, or as good as empty. The bottom of the inside of the bottle was dirtied with something blackish and scaly that also clung a little to the sides.

He wanted to throw the bottle away, but he didn't. He held it in one hand while the fingers of the other cleaned the remaining earth from the outside. When he had cleaned it, he didn't fancy the bottle any more than before; but he dropped it into his pocket. Then he climbed the tractor and started off again.

At that time the sun was high in the sky, and the tractor was working on Whistlers' Hill, which is part of Belper's Farm, fifty yards below Burnt House. As the tractor moved on again, the gulls followed again, rising and falling in their flights, wheeling over the disturbed earth, looking for live things, for food; for good things.

That evening, at tea, Ned Challis brought the bottle out and set it on the table by the loaf of bread. His wife looked at it suspiciously: 'Another of your dirty old things for that museum?'

Ned said: 'It's not museum-stuff. Lisa can have it to take to school. I don't want it.'

Mrs Challis pursed her lips, moved the loaf further away from the bottle, and went to refill the tea-pot.

Lisa took the bottle in her hand. 'Where'd you get it, Dad?'

'Whistlers' Hill. Just below Burnt House.' He frowned suddenly as he spoke, as if he had remembered something.

'What's it got inside?'

'Nothing. And if you try getting the stopper out, that'll break.'

So Lisa didn't try. Next morning she took it to school; but she didn't show it to anyone. Only her cousin Kevin saw it, and that was before school and by accident. He always called for Lisa on his way to school – there was no other company on that country road – and he saw her pick up the bottle from the table, where her mother had left it the night before, and put it into her anorak pocket.

'What was that?' asked Kevin.

'You saw. A little old bottle.'

'Let's see it again – properly.' Kevin was younger than Lisa, and she sometimes indulged him; so she took the bottle out and let him hold it.

At once he tried the stopper.

'Don't,' said Lisa. 'You'll only break it.'

'What's inside?'

'Nothing. Dad found it on Whistlers'.'

'It's not very nice, is it?'

'What do you mean, "Not very nice"?'

'I don't know. But let me keep it for a bit. Please, Lisa.'

On principle Lisa now decided not to give in. 'Certainly not. Give it back.'

He did, reluctantly. 'Let me have it just for today, at school. Please.'

'No.'

'I'll give you something if you'll let me have it. I'll not let anyone else touch it; I'll not let them see it. I'll keep it safe. Just for today.'

'You'd only break it. No. What could you give me, anyway?'

'My week's pocket-money.'

'No. I've said no and I mean no, young Kev.'

'I'd give you that little china dog you like.'

'The one with the china kennel?'

'Yes.'

'The china dog with the china kennel – you'd give me both?'

'Yes.'

'Only for half the day, then,' said Lisa. 'I'll let you have it after school-dinner – look out for me in the playground.

Give it back at the end of school. Without fail. And you be careful with it.'

So the bottle travelled to school in Lisa's anorak pocket, where it bided its time all morning. After school-dinner Lisa met Kevin in the playground and they withdrew together to a corner which was well away from the crowded climbing-frame and the infants' sandpit and the rest. Lisa handed the bottle over. 'At the end of school, mind, without fail. And if we miss each other then,' – for Lisa, being in a higher class, came out of school slightly later than Kevin – 'then you must drop it in at ours as you pass. Promise.'

'Promise.'

They parted. Kevin put the bottle into his pocket. He didn't know why he'd wanted the bottle, but he had. Lots of things were like that. You needed them for a bit; and then you didn't need them any longer.

He had needed this little bottle very much.

He left Lisa and went over to the climbing-frame, where his friends already were. He had set his foot on a rung when he thought suddenly how easy it would be for the glass bottle in his trouser pocket to be smashed against the metal framework. He stepped down again and went over to the fence that separated the playground from the farmland beyond. Tall tussocks of grass grew along it, coming through from the open fields and fringing the very edge of the asphalt. He looked round: Lisa had already gone in, and no one else was watching. He put his hand into his pocket and took it out again with the bottle concealed in the fist. He stooped as if to examine an insect on a tussock, and slipped his hand into the middle of it and left the bottle there, well hidden.

He straightened up and glanced around. Since no one was

looking in his direction, his action had been unobserved; the bottle would be safe. He ran back to the climbing-frame and began to climb, jostling and shouting and laughing, as he and his friends always did. He forgot the bottle.

He forgot the bottle completely.

It was very odd, considering what a fuss he had made about the bottle, that he should have forgotten it; but he did. When the bell rang for the end of playtime, he ran straight in. He did not think of the bottle then, or later. At the end of afternoon school, he did not remember it; and he happened not to see Lisa, who would surely have reminded him.

Only when he was nearly home, and passing the Challises' house, he remembered. He had faithfully promised – and had really meant to keep his promise. But he'd broken it, and left the bottle behind. If he turned and went back to school now, he would meet Lisa, and she would have to be told . . . By the time he got back to the school playground, all his friends would have gone home: the caretaker would be there, and perhaps a late teacher or two, and they'd all want to know what he was up to. And when he'd got the bottle and dropped it in at the Challises', Lisa would scold him all over again. And when he got home at last, he would be very late for his tea, and his mother would be angry.

As he stood by the Challises' gate, thinking, it seemed best, since he had messed things up anyway, to go straight home and leave the bottle to the next day. So he went home.

He worried about the bottle for the rest of the day, without having the time or the quiet to think about it very clearly. He knew that Lisa would assume he had just for-

gotten to leave it at her house on the way home. He half
expected her to turn up after tea, to claim it; but she didn't.
She would have been angry enough about his having forgotten to leave it; but what about her anger tomorrow on the
way to school, when she found that he had forgotten it
altogether – abandoned it in the open playground? He
thought of hurrying straight past her house in the morning;
but he would never manage it. She would be on the lookout.

He saw that he had made the wrong decision earlier. He
ought, at all costs, to have gone back to the playground to
get the bottle.

He went to bed, still worrying. He fell asleep, and his
worry went on, making his dreaming unpleasant in a nagging way. He must be quick, his dreams seemed to nag. *Be
quick* . . .

Suddenly he was wide awake. It was very late. The
sound of the television being switched off must have woken
him. Quietness. He listened to the rest of the family going to
bed. They went to bed and to sleep. Silence. They were all
asleep now, except for him. He couldn't sleep.

Then, as abruptly as if someone had lifted the top of his
head like a lid and popped the idea in, he saw that this time
– almost the middle of the night – was the perfect time for
him to fetch the bottle. He knew by heart the roads between home and school; he would not be afraid. He would
have plenty of time. When he reached the school, the gate to
the playground would be shut, but it was not high: in the
past, by daylight, he and his friends had often climbed it.
He would go into the playground, find the correct tussock
of grass, get the bottle, bring it back, and have it ready to
give to Lisa on the way to school in the morning. She

would be angry, but only moderately angry. She would never know the whole truth.

He got up and dressed quickly and quietly. He began to look for a pocket-torch, but gave up when he realized that would mean opening and shutting drawers and cupboards. Anyway, there was a moon tonight, and he knew his way, and he knew the school playground. He couldn't go wrong.

He let himself out of the house, leaving the door on the latch for his return. He looked at his watch: between a quarter and half past eleven – not as late as he had thought. All the same, he set off almost at a run, but had to settle down into a steady trot. His trotting footsteps on the road sounded clearly in the night quiet. But who was there to hear?

He neared the Challises' house. He drew level with it.

Ned Challis heard. Usually nothing woke him before the alarm-clock in the morning; but tonight footsteps woke him. Who, at this hour – he lifted the back of his wrist towards his face, so that the time glimmered at him – who, at nearly twenty-five to twelve, could be hurrying along that road on foot? When the footsteps had almost gone – when it was already perhaps too late he sprang out of bed and over to the window.

His wife woke. 'What's up, then, Ned?'

'Just somebody. I wondered who.'

'Oh, come back to bed!'

Ned Challis went back to bed; but almost at once got out again.

'Ned! What is it now?'

'I just thought I'd have a look at Lisa.'

At once Mrs Challis was wide awake. 'What's wrong with Lisa?'

'Nothing.' He went to listen at Lisa's door – listen to the regular, healthy breathing of her sleep. He came back. 'Nothing. Lisa's all right.'

'For heaven's sake! Why shouldn't she be?'

'Well, who was it walking out there? Hurrying.'

'Oh, go to sleep!'

'Yes.' He lay down again, drew the bedclothes round him, lay still. But his eyes remained open.

Out in the night, Kevin left the road on which the Challises lived and came into the more important one that would take him into the village. He heard the rumble of a lorry coming up behind him. For safety he drew right into a gateway and waited. The lorry came past at a steady pace, headlights on. For a few seconds he saw the driver and his mate sitting up in the cab, intent on the road ahead. He had not wanted to be noticed by them, but, when they had gone, he felt lonely.

He went on into the village, its houses lightless, its streets deserted. By the entrance to the school driveway, he stopped to make sure he was unobserved. Nobody. Nothing – not even a cat. There was no sound of any vehicle now; but in the distance he heard a dog barking, and then another answered it. A little owl cried and cried for company or for sport. Then that, too, stopped.

He turned into the driveway to the school, and there was the gate to the playground. He looked over it, into the playground. Moonlight showed him everything: the expanse of asphalt, the sandpit, the big climbing-frame, and – at the far end – the fence with the tussocks of grass growing blackly along it. It was all familiar, and yet strange because of the emptiness and the whitening of moonlight and the shadows cast like solid things. The climbing-frame reared high into the air, and on the ground stretched the black criss-cross of its shadows like the bars of a cage.

But he had not come all this way to be halted by moon-shine and insubstantial shadows. In a businesslike way he climbed the gate and crossed the playground to the fence. He wondered whether he would find the right tussock easily, but he did. His fingers closed on the bottle: it was waiting for him.

At that moment, in the Challises' house, as they lay side by side in bed, Mrs Challis said to her husband: 'You're still awake, aren't you?'

'Yes.'

'What is it?'

'Nothing.'

Mrs Challis sighed.

'All right, then,' said Ned Challis. 'It's this. That bottle I gave Lisa – that little old bottle that I gave Lisa yesterday –'

'What about it?'

'I found it by Burnt House.'

Mrs Challis drew in her breath sharply. Then she said, 'That may mean nothing.' Then, 'How near was it?'

'Near enough.' After a pause: 'I ought never to have given it to Lisa. I never thought. But Lisa's all right, any-way.'

'But, Ned, don't you know what Lisa did with that bottle?'

'What?'

'Lent it to Kevin to have at school. And, according to her, he didn't return it when he should have done, on the way home. Didn't you hear her going on and on about it?'

'Kevin . . .' For the third time that night Ned Challis

was getting out of bed, this time putting on his trousers, fumbling for his shoes. 'Somebody went up the road in a hurry. You know – I looked out. I couldn't see properly, but it was somebody small. It could have been a child. It could have been Lisa, but it wasn't. It could well have been Kevin . . .'

'Shouldn't you go to their house first, Ned – find out whether Kevin is there or not? Make sure. You're not sure.'

'I'm not sure. But, if I wait to make sure, I may be too late.'

Mrs Challis did not say, 'Too late for what?' She did not argue.

Ned Challis dressed and went down. As he let himself out of the house to get his bicycle from the shed, the church clock began to strike the hour, the sound reaching him distantly across the intervening fields. He checked with his watch: midnight.

In the village, in the school playground, the striking of midnight sounded clangorously close. Kevin stood with the bottle held in the palm of his hand, waiting for the clock to stop striking – waiting as if for something to follow.

After the last stroke of midnight, there was silence, but Kevin still stood waiting and listening. A car or lorry passed the entrance of the school drive: he heard it distinctly; yet it was oddly faint, too. He couldn't place the oddness of it. It had sounded much further away than it should have done – less really there.

He gripped the bottle and went on listening, as if for some particular sound. The minutes passed. The same dog barked at the same dog, bark and reply – far, unreally far away. The little owl called; from another world, it might have been.

He was gripping the bottle so tightly now that his hand was sweating. He felt his skin begin to prickle with sweat at the back of his neck and under his arms.

Then there was a whistle from across the fields, distantly. It should have been an unexpected sound, just after midnight; but it did not startle him. It did set him off across the playground, however. Too late he wanted to get away. He had to go past the climbing-frame, whose cagework of shadows now stretched more largely than the frame itself. He saw the bars of shadow as he approached; he actually hesitated; and then, like a fool, he stepped inside the cage of shadows.

Ned Challis, on his bicycle, had reached the junction of the by-road with the road that – in one direction – led to the village. In the other it led deeper into the country. Which way? He dismounted. He had to choose the right way – to follow Kevin.

Thinking of Whistlers' Hill, he turned the front wheel of his bicycle away from the village and set off again. But now, with his back to the village, going away from the village, he felt a kind of weariness and despair. A memory of childhood came into his mind: a game he had played in childhood: something hidden for him to find, and if he turned in the wrong direction to search, all the voices whispered to him, 'Cold – cold!' Now, with the village receding behind him, he recognized what he felt: cold . . . cold . . .

Without getting off his bicycle, he wheeled round and began to pedal hard in the direction of the village.

In the playground, there was no pressing hurry for Kevin any more. He did not press against the bars of his cage to get out. Even when clouds cut off the moonlight and the shadows melted into general darkness – even when the shadow-cage was no longer visible to the eye, he stood there; then crouched there, in a corner of the cage, as befitted a prisoner.

The church clock struck the quarter.

The whistlers were in no hurry. The first whistle had come from right across the fields. Then there was a long pause. Then the sound was repeated, equally distantly, from the direction of the river bridges. Later still, another whistle from the direction of the railway line, or somewhere near it.

He lay in his cage, cramped by the bars, listening. He did not know he was thinking, but suddenly it came to him: Whistlers' Hill. He and Lisa and the others had always supposed that the hill had belonged to a family called Whistler, as Challises' house belonged to the Challis family. But that was not how the hill had got its name – he saw that now. No, indeed not.

Whistler answered whistler at long intervals, like the sentries of a besieging army. There was no moving in as yet.

The church clock had struck the quarter as Ned Challis entered the village and cycled past the entrance to the school. He cycled as far as the Recreation Ground, perhaps because that was where Kevin would have gone in the daytime. He cycled bumpily round the Ground: no Kevin.

He began to cycle back the way he had come, as though he had given up altogether and were going home. He cycled slowly. He passed the entrance to the school again.

In this direction, he was leaving the village. He was cycling so slowly that the front wheel of his bicycle wobbled desperately; the light from his dynamo was dim. He put a foot down and stopped. Motionless, he listened. There was nothing to hear, unless – yes, the faintest ghost of a sound, high pitched, prolonged for seconds, remote as from another world. Like a coward – and Ned Challis was no coward – he tried to persuade himself that he had imagined the sound; yet he knew he had not. It came from another direction now: very faint, yet penetrating, so that his skin crinkled to hear it. Again it came, from yet another quarter.

He wheeled his bicycle back to the entrance to the school and left it there. He knew he must be very close. He walked up to the playground gate and peered over it. But the moon was obscured by cloud: he could see nothing. He listened, waited for the moon to sail free.

In the playground Kevin had managed to get up, first on his hands and knees, then upright. He was very much afraid, but he had to be standing to meet whatever it was.

For the whistlers had begun to close in slowly, surely: converging on the school, on the school playground, on the cage of shadows. On him.

For some time now cloud-masses had obscured the moon. He could see nothing; but he felt the whistlers' presence. Their signals came more often, and always closer. Closer. Very close.

Suddenly the moon sailed free.

In the sudden moonlight Ned Challis saw clear across the playground to where Kevin stood against the climbing-frame, with his hands writhing together in front of him.

In the sudden moonlight Kevin did not see his uncle. Between him and the playground gate, and all round him, air was thickening into darkness. Frantically he tried to undo his fingers, that held the little bottle, so that he could throw it from him. But he could not. He held the bottle; the bottle held him.

The darkness was closing in on him. The darkness was about to take him; had surely got him.

Kevin shrieked.

Ned Challis shouted: 'I'm here!' and was over the gate and across the playground and with his arms round the boy: '*I've got you.*'

There was a tinkle as something fell from between Kevin's opened fingers: the little bottle fell and rolled to the middle of the playground. It lay there, very insignificant-looking.

Kevin was whimpering and shaking, but he could move of his own accord. Ned Challis helped him over the gate and to the bicycle.

'Do you think you could sit on the bar, Kev? Could you manage that?'

'Yes.' He could barely speak.

Ned Challis hesitated, thinking of the bottle which had chosen to come to rest in the very centre of the playground, where the first child tomorrow would see it, pick it up.

He went back and picked the bottle up. Wherever he threw it, someone might find it. He might smash it and grind the pieces underfoot; but he was not sure he dared to do that.

Anyway, he was not going to hold it in his hand longer than he strictly must. He put it into his pocket, and then, when he got back to Kevin and the bicycle, he slipped it into the saddle-bag.

He rode Kevin home on the cross-bar of his bicycle. At the Challises' front gate Mrs Challis was waiting, with the dog for company. She just said: 'He all right then?'

'Ah.'

'I'll make a cup of tea while you take him home.'

At his own front door, Kevin said: 'I left the door on the latch. I can get in. I'm all right. I'd rather – I'd rather –'

'Less spoken of, the better,' said his uncle. 'You go to bed. Nothing to be afraid of now.'

He waited until Kevin was inside the house and he heard the latch click into place. Then he rode back to his wife, his cup of tea, and consideration of the problem that lay in his saddle-bag.

After he had told his wife everything, and they had discussed possibilities, Ned Challis said thoughtfully: 'I might take it to the museum, after all. Safest place for it would be inside a glass case there.'

'But you said they wouldn't want it.'

'Perhaps they would, if I told them where I found it and a bit – only a bit – about Burnt House . . .'

'You do that, then.'

Ned Challis stood up and yawned with a finality that said, Bed.

'But don't you go thinking you've solved all your problems by taking that bottle to Castleford, Ned. Not by a long chalk.'

'No?'

'Lisa. She reckons she owns that bottle.'

'I'll deal with Lisa tomorrow.'

'Today, by the clock.'

Ned Challis gave a groan that turned into another yawn. 'Bed first,' he said; 'then Lisa.' They went to bed not long before the dawn.

The next day and for days after that, Lisa was furiously angry with her father. He had as good as stolen her bottle, she said, and now he refused to give it back, to let her see it, even to tell her what he had done with it. She was less angry with Kevin. (She did not know, of course, the circumstances of the bottle's passing from Kevin to her father.)

Kevin kept out of Lisa's way, and even more carefully kept out of his uncle's. He wanted no private conversation.

One Saturday Kevin was having tea at the Challises', because he had been particularly invited. He sat with Lisa and Mrs Challis. Ned had gone to Castleford, and came in late. He joined them at the tea-table in evident good spirits. From his pocket he brought out a small cardboard box, which he placed in the centre of the table, by the Saturday cake. His wife was staring at him: before he spoke, he gave her the slightest nod of reassurance. 'The museum didn't want to keep that little old glass bottle, after all,' he said.

Both the children gave a cry: Kevin started up with such a violent backward movement that his chair clattered to the floor behind him; Lisa leant forward, her fingers clawing towards the box.

'No!' Ned Challis said. To Lisa he added: 'There it stays, girl, till *I* say.' To Kevin: 'Calm down. Sit up at the table again and listen to me.' Kevin picked his chair up and sat down again, resting his elbows on the table, so that his hands supported his head.

'Now,' said Ned Challis, 'you two know so much that it's probably better you should know more. That little old bottle came from Whistlers' Hill, below Burnt House – well, you know that. Burnt House is only a ruin now – elder bushes growing inside as well as out; but once it was a cottage that someone lived in. Your mother's granny remembered the last one to live there.'

'No, Ned,' said Mrs Challis, 'it was my great-granny remembered.'

'Anyway,' said Ned Challis, 'it was so long ago that

Victoria was the Queen, that's certain. And an old woman lived alone in that cottage. There were stories about her.'

'Was she a witch?' breathed Lisa.

'So they said. They said she went out on the hillside at night –'

'At the full of the moon,' said Mrs Challis.

'They said she dug up roots and searched out plants and toadstools and things. They said she caught rats and toads and even bats. They said she made ointments and powders and weird brews. And they said she used what she made to cast spells and call up spirits.'

'Spirits from Hell, my great-granny said. Real bad 'uns.'

'So people said, in the village. Only the parson scoffed at the whole idea. Said he'd called often and been shown over the cottage and seen nothing out of the ordinary – none of the jars and bottles of stuff that she was supposed to have for her witchcraft. He said she was just a poor cranky old woman; that was all.

'Well, she grew older and older and crankier and crankier, and one day she died. Her body lay in its coffin in the cottage, and the parson was going to bury her next day in the churchyard.

'The night before she was to have been buried, someone went up from the village –'

'Someone!' said Mrs Challis scornfully. 'Tell them the whole truth, Ned, if you're telling the story at all. Half the village went up, with lanterns – men, women, and children. Go on, Ned.'

'The cottage was thatched, and they began to pull swatches of straw away and take it into the cottage and strew it round and heap it up under the coffin. They were going to fire it all.

'They were pulling the straw on the downhill side of the cottage when suddenly a great piece of thatch came away and out came tumbling a whole lot of things that the old woman must have kept hidden there. People did hide things in thatches, in those days.'

'Her savings?' asked Lisa.

'No. A lot of jars and little bottles, all stoppered or sealed, neat and nice. With stuff inside.'

There was a silence at the tea-table. Then Lisa said: 'That proved it: she was a witch.'

'Well, no, it only proved she *thought* she was a witch. That was what the parson said afterwards – and whew! was he mad when he knew about that night.'

Mrs Challis said: 'He gave it 'em red hot from the pulpit the next Sunday. He said that once upon a time poor old deluded creatures like her had been burnt alive for no reason at all, and the village ought to be ashamed of having burnt her dead.'

Lisa went back to the story of the night itself. 'What did they do with what came out of the thatch?'

'Bundled it inside the cottage among the straw, and fired it all. The cottage burnt like a beacon that night, they say. Before cockcrow, everything had been burnt to ashes. That's the end of the story.'

'Except for my little bottle,' said Lisa. 'That came out of the thatch, but it didn't get picked up. It rolled downhill, or someone kicked it.'

'That's about it,' Ned agreed.

Lisa stretched her hand again to the cardboard box, and this time he did not prevent her. But he said: 'Don't be surprised, Lisa. It's different.'

She paused. 'A different bottle?'

'The same bottle, but – well, you'll see.'

Lisa opened the box, lifted the packaging of cotton wool, took the bottle out. It was the same bottle, but the stopper had gone, and it was empty and clean – so clean that it shone greenly. Innocence shone from it.

'You said the stopper would never come out,' Lisa said slowly.

'They forced it by suction. The museum chap wanted to know what was inside, so he got the hospital lab to take a look – he has a friend there. It was easy for them.'

Mrs Challis said: 'That would make a pretty vase, Lisa. For tiny flowers.' She coaxed Lisa to go out to pick a posy from the garden; she herself took the bottle away to fill it with water.

Ned Challis and Kevin faced each other across the table.

Kevin said: 'What was in it?'

Ned Challis said: 'A trace of this, a trace of that, the hospital said. One thing more than anything else.'

'Yes?'

'Blood. Human blood.'

Lisa came back with her flowers; Mrs Challis came back with the bottle filled with water. When the flowers had been put in, it looked a pretty thing.

'My witch-bottle,' said Lisa contentedly. 'What was she called – the old woman that thought she was a witch?'

Her father shook his head; her mother thought: 'Madge – or was it Maggy –?'

'Maggy Whistler's bottle, then,' said Lisa.

'Oh, no,' said Mrs Challis. 'She was Maggy – or Madge – Dawson. I remember my granny saying so. Dawson.'

'Then why's it called Whistlers' Hill?'

'I'm not sure,' said Mrs Challis uneasily. 'I mean, I don't think anyone knows for certain.'

But Ned Challis, looking at Kevin's face, knew that he knew for certain.

Miss Mountain

WHATEVER else might be spring-cleaned in Grandmother's house, it was never her box-room. Old Mrs Robinson lived in a house with only two rooms upstairs, besides the bathroom: one was her bedroom; the other the box-room. This room fascinated her grandchildren, Daisy and Jim. It was about eight feet by six, and so full of stuff that even to open the door properly was difficult. If you forced it open enough to poke your head round, you saw a positive mountain of things reaching almost to the ceiling – old suitcases, bulging cardboard boxes of all shapes and sizes, stringed up parcels of magazines, cascades of old curtains, and a worm-eaten chair or two.

Grandmother was teased about the state of her box-room. She retorted with spirit: 'There isn't as much stuff as there seems to be, because it's all piled up on the spare bed. The room's really a guest-room. I'm only waiting for a bit of time to clear it.'

Then everybody would laugh – Daisy and Jim and their father, who was Grandmother's son, and their mother, who was her daughter-in-law. Grandmother would join in the laughter. She always laughed a lot, even at herself.

If they went on to suggest lending a hand in the clearing of the box-room, Grandmother stopped laughing to say: 'I'd rather do it myself, thank you, when I have a bit of time.' But she never seemed to have that bit.

She was the nicest of grandmothers: rosy to look at, and

plump, and somehow cosy. She liked to spoil her grand-children. Daisy and Jim lived on an estate only just round the corner from Grandmother's little house, so they were always calling on her, and she on them.

Then suddenly everything was going to change.

The children's father got another job that would mean the whole family's moving out of the district, leaving Grandmother behind.

'Goodness me!' Grandmother said, cheerful about most things. 'It isn't the end of the world! I can come and visit you for the day.'

'Not just for the day,' said young Mrs Robinson, who was very fond of her mother-in-law. 'You must come and stay – often.'

'And the children shall come and stay with me,' Grandmother said.

'Where shall we sleep?' Jim asked.

'You'll have to clear the guest-room,' Daisy said.

'Yes, of course,' said her grandmother, but for a moment looked as if she had not quite foreseen that, and regretted the whole idea. But really the clearing out of the box-room ought to have been done years and years ago.

Grandmother said that she preferred to do all the work herself; but everyone insisted that it would be too much for her. In the end she agreed to let Daisy and Jim help her. Perhaps she thought they would be easier to manage than their parents.

How much the box-room held was amazing; and every-thing had to be brought out and sorted carefully. A lot went straight into the dustbin; some things – such as the bundles of magazines and the curtaining – went to the Church Hall for the next jumble sale; the chairs went onto the bonfire.

Grandmother went through all the suitcases and got rid of everything; the suitcases themselves were only fit for jumble. The cardboard boxes, Grandmother said, were going to be more difficult; so for the moment they were piled up in a corner of her bedroom.

They sorted and cleared for several days. Sure enough, under the mountain, there really had been a bed – narrow, but quite wide enough for Daisy (who was older and larger than Jim), and there was a mattress on it, and pillows and blankets (only one moth-eaten enough for the dustbin). Grandmother made the bed up at once with sheets and pillowcases from her airing-cupboard.

'There!' she said. 'My guest-room!'

Daisy and Jim loved it. The room seemed so small and private, with an old-fashioned wallpaper that must have been there before Grandmother moved in, all those years ago. The window looked over the garden and received the morning sun. (Of course, that meant that in the evening the room dimmed early.)

All that remained was to clear the cardboard boxes still in Grandmother's own bedroom. She said she could do this herself in the evening when the children had gone home. But Daisy thought her grandmother already looked tired. She made her sit down in a chair, and the two children began going through the boxes for her. 'We'll show you everything as we come to it,' Daisy said.

Grandmother sighed.

For the first half hour, everything went out to the dustbin – the cardboard boxes themselves and their contents, which turned out to be certificates of this and that and old programmes and views and other souvenirs. Then they came to boxes of photographs, some of them framed. These delayed the children.

'Look, Daisy!' said Jim. 'What a fat little girl!'

'Here she is again,' said Daisy. 'Just a bit older and even fatter.'

'It's me,' said their grandmother, and leant forward from her chair to dart a hand between the two children and take the photographs and tear them in halves as rubbish.

'Grandmother!' they protested; but it was too late.

They found a framed wedding group of long ago with

gentlemen in high-buttoning jackets and ladies wearing long dresses and hats toppling with feathers and flowers and fruit and bows.

'Was this your wedding, Grandmother?'

Grandmother said: 'I'm not as old as *that*. I wasn't thought of then. That was the wedding of my mother and father.'

The children peered. 'So that's our great-grandfather and our great-grandmother . . .'

'And a couple of your great great aunts as bridesmaids,' said their grandmother. She snorted. 'I preferred not to go in for bridesmaids.' She found them a photograph of her own wedding, with everybody still looking very strange and old-fashioned, but clearly their grandmother did not think so.

The children thought that the quaint wedding group of their great grandparents would suit the little guest-room. With their grandmother's agreement, they hung it there. All the other photographs went down to the dustbin.

The last of the cardboard boxes was a squarish one, from which Daisy now drew out a barrel-shaped container. The staves of the barrel and the bands encircling them, and the lid, were all of the same tarnished metal.

Grandmother said: 'That's a biscuit barrel.'

'Is it real silver?' asked Daisy.

'Yes,' said Grandmother.

'How grand!' said Jim.

'Yes,' said Grandmother. 'Very valuable.'

Daisy set the biscuit barrel respectfully on the floor where they could all admire it.

'It was in our house when I was a child,' said Grandmother. 'I never liked it.'

'There's a curly H on it,' said Jim.

'For Hill,' said Grandmother. 'That was our surname. But I hated that biscuit barrel. I've always meant to get rid of it.'

'Please, Grandmother!' cried Daisy. 'You could stand it on the sideboard downstairs. It would look so nice. I'll polish up the silver.' Their grandmother still stared unforgivingly at the barrel. 'Think, Grandmother: you could keep biscuits in it for when we come to stay. Our favourite biscuits. I like custard-creams best.'

'I like pink sugar wafers,' said Jim.

'Promise you'll keep it, Grandmother, to keep our biscuits in,' said Daisy.

Grandmother stopped looking at the biscuit barrel and looked at her grandchildren instead. Suddenly she jumped up to hug them. 'Oh, yes!' she said. 'For, after all, I'm lucky. Very, very lucky. I've a guest-room and two grand-children who want to come and stay with me!'

The little guest-room, so small and private, was ready for its first guest.

The first guest was Jim. Perhaps by rights it should have been Daisy, because she was the elder, but Jim was the one likely to be a nuisance during the family's house-removal. So the night before the removal, and the first night after the removal were spent by Jim in his grandmother's guest-room. Then his father drove over and fetched him back to their new home.

In the new house, everyone was tired with the work of getting straight, and might have been short-tempered with Jim's little-boy bounciness. But Jim was quieter than usual. They asked whether he had had a good time with his grandmother. Yes, he had gone shopping with her, and she had bought him a multi-coloured pen; and he had had sparklers in the garden after dark; and peaches for both his suppers; and Grandmother had had pink sugar wafer biscuits for him – his favourite.

'You're lucky to have a grandmother like that,' said his mother.

'Reminds me of my own granny,' said his father, 'your grandmother's mother. She was a good sort, too.'

That night Daisy and Jim had to share a bedroom, because Daisy's room wasn't ready yet. Jim went to bed, and asked his mother to leave the landing light on and the door ajar. 'I thought you'd given that up,' she said. 'You're a big boy now.' But she let him have his way.

Later, when Daisy came up, he was still awake.

Daisy said: 'I'll be in my own room tomorrow night.'

'I don't mind sharing.'

Daisy got into bed.

'Daisy . . .'

'What?'

'I don't want to sleep here alone tomorrow night.'

'But – but, Jim, you always sleep alone!' There was no reply from the other bed. 'Jim, you're just being silly!'

Still no reply; and yet a little noise. Daisy listened carefully: Jim was crying.

She got out of bed and went to him. 'What is it?'

'Nothing.'

'It must be something.'

'No, it's not. It's nothing.'

Daisy knew Jim. He could be very obstinate. Perhaps he would never tell her about whatever it was.

'You'd feel better if you told me, Jim.'

'No, I shouldn't.'

He was crying so much that she put her arms round him. It struck her that he was shivering.

'Are you cold, Jim?'

'No.'

'Then why are you shivering? You're not afraid of something?'

In answer, Jim gave a kind of gasp. 'Let me alone.'

Daisy was extremely irritated – and curious, too. 'Go on – say something. I shan't let you alone till you say something.'

Still he did not speak; and Daisy amended: 'If you say something, I won't argue – I'll go back to bed and let you alone. But you must say something – something that *is* something.'

Jim collected himself; said carefully: 'I don't want to stay the night in Grandmother's house again – ever.' He turned over in bed with his back to Daisy.

Daisy stared at him, opened her mouth, remembered her promise, shut it, went back to bed and lay there to think. She tried to think what might have happened during Jim's visit to make him feel as he did. It occurred to her that she might find out when her turn for a visit came . . .

How odd of Jim. There could be nothing to be afraid of at night in the house of the cosiest, rosiest, plumpest of grandmothers.

The moment she fell asleep, she was standing on her grandmother's front doorstep, her suitcase in her hand. She had already knocked. The door opened just as usual; there stood her grandmother, just as usual. But no, not as usual. Her grandmother peered at Daisy as if at a stranger. 'Yes?' she said. 'I'm Daisy Robinson,' said Daisy. 'I'm your granddaughter. I've come to stay the night.' Without a word, her grandmother stood aside to let her enter. At once Daisy began to mount the stairs that led to that early-shadowed little guest-room. She already saw the door ajar, waiting for her. Behind her, downstairs, she could hear her grandmother securing the front door for the night – the lock, the bolts, the chain: she shut the two of them in together for the night. Daisy could hear her grandmother's little laugh: she was chuckling to herself.

The rest of the dream – if there were any – had vanished by the time Daisy woke in the morning. All she knew of it was that she was glad she could not remember it.

Daisy told no one about Jim, chiefly because there was so little to tell. He seemed all right again, anyway. By that evening the bedrooms had been sorted out, so that Jim had his to himself. Without protest, he went to sleep alone. It's true that he screamed in the night, so that his mother had to go to him, but all children have nightmares sometimes. By the next night he had resumed his usual sound sleeping.

So Jim had been making a strange fuss about nothing, Daisy thought; or perhaps he'd got used to the idea of whatever there might have been; or – not the most comfortable idea for Daisy – he had been able to shut it from his mind because he was now a safe distance from Grandmother's little guest-room.

Their grandmother came to stay. She was her usual cheerful self, and everyone enjoyed the visit; Jim seemed to enjoy her company as much as usual. At the end of her visit, Grandmother said, 'Well, which of you two is coming to sleep in my guest-room next?'

Jim said: 'It's Daisy's turn.'

'That's very fair of you, Jim,' their mother said approvingly. Daisy looked at Jim; but Jim stubbornly looked past her. She knew that he would not have agreed to go under any circumstances.

Only a few weeks later, Daisy went.

With her suitcase, she stood on her grandmother's door-step. Twice she raised a hand to the knocker, and twice let it fall. The third time, she really knocked. She heard the patter of her grandmother's feet approaching. The door opened, and there was Grandmother, and all the uneasy feelings that Jim had given her vanished away. Her grand-mother was laughing for joy at her coming, and the house seemed to welcome her. Even from the doorway Daisy could see into the sitting-room, where the electric light had not yet been switched on: an open fire burned brightly, and by the fireplace stood a tea-table with the china on it shin-ing in the firelight, and beyond that glowed the polish of the sideboard with the objects on it all giving as much glow or glitter as they could.

They had tea with boiled eggs and salad, as time was getting on and this had to be tea and supper together.

'Anything more you fancy, Daisy, dear?'

Daisy looked over to the sideboard, to the biscuit barrel. 'Pink sugar wafers?' she said.

'What an idea!' said her grandmother. 'They're not *your* favourite biscuits!'

Daisy went over to the biscuit barrel, put her hand in. 'Go on, dear, take whatever you find, as many as you want. I like you to do that.'

Daisy drew out a custard-cream biscuit. 'Grandmother, you're wonderful! You never forget anything.'

Grandmother sighed. 'Sometimes I wish I were more forgetful.'

Daisy laughed, and munched.

Later, they went to bed. They stood side by side looking into the little guest-room. With the curtains drawn and the bedside light glowing from inside a pink shade, the room looked as cosy and rosy as Grandmother herself. 'I hope you sleep well, my dear,' said her grandmother, and talked about the number of blankets and the number of pillows and the possibility of noise from neighbouring houses. Sometimes people had late parties.

'Did the neighbours disturb Jim?' Daisy asked suddenly.

'No,' said her grandmother. 'At least – he's a poor sleeper for such a young child, isn't he? He slept badly here.'

Daisy glanced sideways to see her grandmother's expression when she had said this. She found her grandmother stealing a sideways glance at her. They both looked away at once, pretending nothing had happened.

'Remember,' said Grandmother, 'if you want anything, I'm just across the landing.' She kissed Daisy good night.

Daisy decided not to think about that sideways glance tonight. She went to bed, slipped easily downhill into sleep, and slept.

Something woke her. She wasn't sure that it had been a noise, but surely it must have been. She lay very still, her eyes open, her ears listening. Before going to bed, she had drawn the curtains back, so that she would wake to the morning sun: now it was night, without moon or stars, and all the lights of the surrounding houses had been extinguished.

She waited to hear a repetition of noise in the house; but there was none. She knew what she was expecting to hear: the creak of a stair-tread. There was nothing; but she became sure, all the same, that someone was creeping downstairs.

It could be – it *must* be – her grandmother going downstairs for something. She would go quietly, for fear of waking Daisy. But would she manage to go so very, very quietly?

Whoever it was would have reached the foot of the stairs by now. Still no noise.

It must be her grandmother; and yet Daisy felt that it wasn't her grandmother. And yet again she felt it was her grandmother.

She must know. She called 'Grandmother!', pitching her voice rather high to reach the bottom of the stairs. The sound she made came out scream-like.

Almost at once she heard her grandmother's bedroom door open and the quick, soft sound of her feet bringing her across to the guest-room.

'Here I am, dear!'

'I thought I heard – I thought you were going downstairs, Grandmother.'

Grandmother seemed – well, agitated. 'Oh, did you? Sometimes I need a drink of water in the night, and sometimes I do go downstairs for it.'

'But it wasn't you. You came from your bedroom just now, not back up the stairs.'

'What sharp ears you have, dear!'

'I didn't exactly *hear* anyone going downstairs, anyway,' Daisy said slowly.

'So it was all a mistake. That's all right then, isn't it?'

Not a mistake; more of a muddle, Daisy thought. But she let herself be kissed good night again, and her light was switched off. Her grandmother went back to bed. There was quiet in the house: not only no unusual sound, but no feel of anything unusual. Daisy slept until morning sunshine.

The daytime was made as delightful for Daisy as her grandmother had made it for Jim. But evening came, and night; and this night was far worse than the previous one.

Daisy woke, and lay awake, knowing that someone was creeping downstairs again. But it's my imagination, she told herself; how can I know, when I hear nothing?

Whoever it was reached the bottom of the stairs and crossed the hall to the sitting-room door. Had Grandmother left that door shut or open when she went to bed? It did not matter. Whoever it was had entered the sitting-room and was moving across to the sideboard.

What was happening down there in the dark and the silence?

Suddenly there was no more silence. From downstairs there was a shrill scream, that turned into a crying and sobbing, both terrified and terrifying.

Hardly knowing what she was doing, Daisy was out of bed, through her bedroom door, across the landing to her grandmother's room. The door was shut: she had to pause an instant to open it, and in that instant she realized that the crying from downstairs had stopped.

She was inside her grandmother's bedroom. The bedside light was on and Grandmother, flustered, had just sat up in bed. Daisy said: 'That crying!'

'It was me,' said her grandmother.

'Oh, no, no, no, no!' Daisy contradicted her grandmother with fury. She glared at her in fury and terror: the nicest grandmother in the world was concealing something, lying. What kind of grandmother was she then: sly; perhaps treacherous? Wicked?

At the look on Daisy's face, Grandmother shrank back among the pillows. She hid her face in her hands. Between the fingers Daisy saw tears beginning to roll down over the dry old skin. Grandmother was crying, with gasping sobs, and her crying was not all that different, but much quieter, from the crying Daisy had heard downstairs.

In the middle of her crying, Grandmother managed to say, 'Oh, Daisy!' and stretched out her hands towards her, begging her.

Daisy looked searchingly at her grandmother; and her grandmother met her gaze. Daisy took the outstretched hands and stroked them. She calmed herself even while she calmed her grandmother. 'I'll make us a pot of tea,' she said. 'I'll bring it up here.'

'No,' said her grandmother. 'I'll come down. We'll have it downstairs, and I'll tell you – I'll tell you –' She began to cry again.

Daisy was no longer afraid. She went downstairs into the kitchen to boil a kettle. As she went, she turned the sitting-room light on, and switched on an electric fire. Everything was exactly as usual. The door had been shut.

From downstairs she heard her grandmother getting up and then coming out of her bedroom. She did not come directly downstairs: Daisy heard her cross the landing into the guest-room, spend a few moments there, then come down.

Daisy carried the tea on a tray into the sitting-room; she took the biscuit barrel off the sideboard and put it on the tray, in case Grandmother wanted something to eat with her tea. Grandmother was already waiting for her. She had

brought downstairs with her the framed wedding photograph from Daisy's bedroom, and set it where they could
both see it. Daisy asked no question.

They sat together and sipped their tea. Daisy also
nibbled a biscuit; her grandmother had shaken her head
and shuddered when Daisy offered her the biscuit barrel.

'Now I'll tell you,' said Grandmother. She paused,
while she steadied herself, visibly. 'I brought the wedding
photo down so that I could *show* you.'

Again she paused, for much longer; so Daisy said, 'Your
mother looked sweet as a bride.'

'I never knew her,' said Grandmother. 'She died when I
was very young.'

Daisy said, 'But Dad knew her! He talks about his
granny.'

'That was my stepmother; his step-grandmother.'

Now something seemed plain to Daisy. 'A stepmother –
poor Grandmother!'

'No,' said Grandmother. 'It wasn't like that at all. My
stepmother – only I never really think of her as my stepmother, just as my mother – she was a darling.'

'Then –?'

'They're both in the group,' said Grandmother. 'My
mother as the bride. My stepmother – as she later became –
as one of the bridesmaids. The bridesmaids were my two
aunts: one my mother's sister, whom my father married
after my mother's death; the other my father's sister.'

Daisy studied the photograph. Now that she knew
that one of the bridesmaids was the bride's sister, it was
easy to see which: there was the same plumpness with
prettiness.

The other bridesmaid was tall, thin, and rather glum-looking. There was a resemblance between her and the bridegroom, but not such a striking one.

'When my mother died,' said Grandmother, 'I was a very little girl, still babyish in my ways, no doubt. My father had to get someone to look after me and to run the house. He was in business and away at his office all day.

'He asked his sister to come – the other bridesmaid.'

Daisy looked at the thin bridesmaid, and wondered.

'She'd always been very fond of my father, I believe, and jealous of his having married. Perhaps she was glad that my mother had died; perhaps she would have been glad if I had never been born. She would have had my father all to herself then.

'She hated me.'

'Grandmother!'

'Oh, yes, she hated me. I didn't fully understand it then. I just thought I had suddenly become stupid and disobedient and dirty and everything that – as it seemed to me – anyone would hate. I daresay I was rather a nasty little girl: I became so. One of the worst things was –'

Grandmother stopped speaking, shaded her face with her hand.

'Go on.'

'It won't seem terrible to you. You may just laugh. Aunt used to sneer. When she sneered, that made it worse.'

'But what was it?'

'I ate.'

'Well, but . . .'

'I ate whenever I could. I ate enormously at meals, and I ate between meals. Aunt used to point it out to my father, and put a tape-measure round where she said my waist should be, as I sat at table. I've always been plump, like my mother's side of the family: I grew fat – terribly fat.

'Our surname was Hill. There were two Miss Hills in the house, my aunt and myself. But Aunt said there need be no confusion: she was Miss Hill; I was Miss Mountain. She called me Miss Mountain, unless my father were present. She would leave notes to me, addressed to Miss Mountain. Once my father found one and asked her about it, and she pretended it was just a little joke between us. But it wasn't a joke – or if it were, it was a cruel, cruel one.'

'Couldn't you just have eaten less and grown thinner and spoilt her game?' asked Daisy.

'You don't understand. Her teasing of me made me eat even more. I took to stealing food. I'd slip out to the larder after Sunday dinner and tear the crisp bits of fat off the joint while it was still warm. Or I'd take sultanas out of the jar in the store-cupboard. Or I'd pare off bits of cheese. Even a slice of dry bread, if there were nothing else. Once I ate dog-biscuits from the shelf above the kennel.

'Of course, sooner or later, Aunt realized what was happening. She began to expect it, and took a delight in catching me out. If she couldn't catch me at it, she would prevent me. She took to locking the kitchen door at night, because she knew I went down then to the store-cupboard and larder.

'Then I found the biscuit barrel.'

'This very biscuit barrel?'

'Yes. It always stood on the sideboard with cream crackers in it – just the plainest of biscuits, to be eaten with cheese. Well, I didn't mind that. I used to creep down for a cream cracker or two in the middle of the night.'

'In this house?'

'Goodness, no! We lived a hundred miles from here, and the house has been pulled down now, I believe.

'Anyway, I used to creep down, as I've said. I daren't put on any light, although I was terribly afraid of the dark – I had become afraid of so many things by then. I felt my way into the room and across to the sideboard, and along it. The sideboard was rather grand, with a mirror, and all kinds of grand utensils were kept on it: the silver cream jug, a pair of silver candlesticks, the silver-rimmed bread board with the silver-handled bread-knife. I felt among them until I found the biscuit barrel. Then I took off the lid and put my hand in.'

She paused.

'Go on, Grandmother.'

'I did that trip once, twice, perhaps three times. The third or fourth time seemed just as usual. As usual, I was shaking with fright, both at the crime I was committing and at the blackness in which I had to commit it. I had felt my way to the biscuit barrel. I lifted the lid with my left hand, as usual. Very carefully, as usual, I slipped my right hand into the barrel. I had thought there would be crackers to the top; but there were not. I had to reach towards the bottom – down – down – down – and then my fingers touched something and at once there was something – oh, it seemed like an explosion! – something snapped at me, caught my fingers, held them in a bitter grip, causing me pain, but far more than pain: terror. I screamed and screamed and sobbed and cried.

'Footsteps came hurrying down the stairs, lights appeared, people were rushing into the dining-room, where I was. My father, my aunt, the maidservant – they all stood looking at me, a fat little girl in her nightdress, screaming,

47

with her right hand extended and a mouse-trap dangling from the fingers.

'My father and the servant were bewildered; but I could see that my aunt was not taken by surprise. She had been expecting this, waiting for it. Now she burst into loud laughter. I couldn't bear it. With my left hand I caught up the silver-handled bread-knife from the sideboard and I went for her.'

'You killed her?'

'No, of course not. I was in such a muddle with screaming and crying, and the knife was in my left hand, and my aunt side-stepped, and my father rushed in and took hold of me and took the knife from me. Then he prised the mouse-trap off my other hand.

'All this time I never stopped crying. I think I was deliberately crying myself ill. Through my crying I heard my father and my aunt talking, and I heard my father asking my aunt how there came to be a mouse-trap inside the biscuit barrel.

'The next day either I was ill or I pretended to be – there wasn't much difference, anyway. I stayed all day in bed with the curtains drawn. The maid brought me bread and milk to eat. My aunt did not come to see me. My father came, in the morning before he went to his office, and in the evening when he got home. On both occasions I pretended to be asleep.

'The day after that I got up. The fingers of my right hand were still red where the trap had snapped across them, and I rubbed them to make them even redder. I didn't want to be well. I showed them to the maidservant. Not only were the fingers red, but two of the finger-nails had gone quite black. The maid called my father in – he

was just on his way to work. He said that the doctor should
see them, and the maid could take me there that afternoon
on foot. Exercise would do me good, and change. He
looked at me as if he were about to say more, but he did not.
He did not mention my aunt – who would have been the

person to take me to see the doctor, ordinarily – and there was still no sign of her.

'The maid took me. The doctor said my fingers had been badly bruised by the blow of the mousetrap, but nothing worse. The finger-nails would grow right. I was disappointed. I had hoped that my finger bones were broken, that my fingertips would drop off. I wanted to be sent into hospital. I didn't want to go home and be well and go on as before: little Miss Mountain as before.

'I walked home with the maid.

'As we neared our house, I saw a woman turn in at our gateway. When we reached the gate, she was walking up the long path to the front door. Now I've said I never knew my own mother, to remember; but when I saw the back-view of that young woman – she *stumped* along a little, as stoutish people often do – I knew that that was exactly what my mother had looked like. I didn't think beyond that; that was enough for me. I ran after her, as fast as I could; and, as she reached the front door, I ran into her. She lost her balance, she gave a cry between alarm and laughter, and sat down suddenly on the front doorstep, and I tumbled on top of her, and felt her arms round me, and burrowed into her, among the folds of all the clothing that women wore in those days. I always remember the plump softness and warmth of her body, and how sweet it was. I cried and cried for joy, and she hugged me.

'That was my other aunt, the other bridesmaid – my mother's sister. My father had telegraphed for her to come, from the other side of England, and she had come. My father had already sent my thin aunt packing – I never saw her again. My plump aunt moved in as housekeeper, and our house was filled with laughter and happiness and love.

Within the year, my father had married her. She had no child of her own by him, so I was her only child. She loved me, and I her.'

'Did you – did you manage to become less stout?' Daisy asked delicately.

'I suppose I must have done. Anyway, I stopped stealing food. And the biscuit barrel disappeared off the sideboard – my new mother put it away, after she'd heard the story, I suppose. Out of sight, out of mind: I forgot it. Or at least I pretended to myself that I'd forgotten it. But whenever it turns up, I remember. I remember too well.'

'I've heard of haunted houses,' said Daisy thoughtfully. 'But never of a haunted biscuit barrel. I don't think it would be haunted if you weren't there to remember, you know.'

'I daresay.'

'Will you get rid of it, Grandmother? Otherwise Jim will never come to stay again; and I – I –'

'You don't think I haven't wanted to get rid of it, child?' cried her grandmother. 'Your grandfather wouldn't let me; your father wouldn't let me. But, no – that was never the real explanation. Then, I couldn't bring myself to give them my reasons – to tell the whole story; and so the memory has held me, like a trap. Now I've told the story; now I'm free; now the biscuit barrel can go.'

'Will you sell it, Grandmother? It must be worth a lot of money.'

'No doubt.'

'I wonder how much money you'll get; and what you'll spend it on, Grandmother . . .'

Grandmother did not answer.

The next morning Daisy woke to sunshine and the

sound of her Grandmother already up and about down-stairs. Daisy dressed quickly and went down. The front door was wide open and her grandmother stood outside on the doorstep, looking at something further up the street. There was the sound of a heavy vehicle droning its way slowly along the street, going away.

Daisy joined her grandmother on the doorstep, and looked where she was looking. The weekly dustbin van was droning its way along: it had almost reached the end of the street. The men were slinging into it the last of the rubbish that the householders had put out for them overnight or early this morning. The two rows of great metal teeth at the back of the van opened and closed slowly, mercilessly on whatever had been thrown into that huge maw.

Grandmother said: 'There it goes;' and at once Daisy knew what 'it' was. 'Done up in a plastic bag with my empty bottles and tins and the old fish-finger carton and broken eggshells and I don't know what rubbish else. Bad company – serve it right.' The van began to turn the cor-ner. 'I've hated it,' said Grandmother. 'And now it's being scrunched to pieces. Smashed to smithereens.' Fiercely she spoke; and Daisy remembered the little girl who had snatched up a breadknife in anger.

The van had turned the corner.

Gone.

Grandmother put her arm round Daisy and laughed. She said: 'Daisy, dear, always remember that one can keep custard-creams and pink sugar wafers for friends in any old tin.'

Guess

THAT last day of October a freak storm hit the suburb of Woodley Park. Slates rattled off roofs, dustbins chased dustbin lids along the streets, hoardings were slammed down, and at midnight there was a huge sound like a giant breaking his kindling wood, and then an almighty crash, and then briefly the sound of the same giant crunching his toast.

Then only the wind, which died surprisingly soon.

In the morning everyone could see that the last forest tree of Grove Road – of the whole suburb – had fallen, crashing down on to Grove Road Primary School. No lives had been lost, since the caretaker did not live on the premises; but the school hamster had later to be treated for shock. The school buildings were wrecked.

Everyone went to stare, especially, of course, the children of the school. They included Netty and Sid Barr.

The fallen tree was an awesome sight, partly because of its size and partly because of its evident great age. Someone in the crowd said that the acorn that grew into *that* must have been planted centuries ago.

As well as the confusion of fallen timber on the road and on the school premises, there was an extraordinary spatter of school everywhere: slates off the roof, bricks from the broken walls, glass from the windows, and the contents of classrooms, cloakrooms and storerooms – books and collages and clay and paints and Nature tables and a queer mixture of clothing, both dingy and weird, which meant that the contents of the Lost Property cupboard and the dressing-up cupboard had been whirled together and tossed outside. Any passer-by could have taken his pick, free of charge. Netty Barr, who had been meaning to claim her gym-shoes from Lost Property, decided that they had gone for good now. This was like the end of the world – a school world.

Council workmen arrived with gear to cut, saw, and haul timber. Fat old Mr Brown from the end of the Barrs' road told the foreman that they ought to have taken the tree down long ago. Perhaps he was right. In spite of last season's leaves and next year's buds, the trunk of the tree was quite hollow: a cross-section revealed a rim of wood the width of a man's hand, encircling a space large enough for a child or a smallish adult. As soon as the workmen's backs were turned, Sid Barr crept in. He then managed to get stuck and had to be pulled out by Netty. An untidy young woman near by was convulsed with silent laughter at the incident.

'You didn't stay inside for a hundred years,' she said to Sid.

'That smelt funny,' said Sid. 'Rotty.' Netty banged his clothes for him: the smell clung.

'Remember that day last summer, Net? After the picnic? When I got stuck inside that great old tree in Epping Forest?' Sid liked to recall near-disasters.

'Epping Forest?' said the young woman, sharply interested. But no one else was.

Meanwhile the headmaster had arrived, and that meant all fun was over. School would go on, after all, even if not in these school-buildings for the time being. The pupils of **Grove Road** were marshalled and then sent off in groups to

various other schools in the neighbourhood. Netty and Sid
Barr, with others, went to Stokeside School: Netty in the
top class, Sid in a lower one.

There was a good deal of upheaval in Netty's new classroom before everyone had somewhere to sit. Netty was the
next-to-last to find a place; the last was a thin, pale girl who
chose to sit next to Netty. Netty assumed that she was a
Stokesider; yet there was something familiar about her,
too. Perhaps she'd just seen her about. The girl had dark,
lank hair gathered into a pony-tail of sorts, and a pale
pointed face with greyish-green eyes. She wore a dingy
green dress that looked ready for a jumble sale, and gym-
shoes.

Netty studied her sideways. At last, 'You been at
Stokeside long?' Netty asked.

The other girl shook her head and glanced at the teacher,
who was talking. She didn't seem to want to talk; but Netty
did.

'A tree fell on our school,' whispered Netty. The other
girl laughed silently, although Netty could see nothing to
laugh about. She did see something, however: this girl bore
a striking resemblance to the young woman who had
watched Sid being pulled from the hollow tree-trunk. The
silent laughter clinched the resemblance.

Of course, this girl was much, much younger. Of
course.

'How old are you?' whispered Netty.

The girl said a monosyllable, still looking amused.

'What did you say?'

Clearly now: 'Guess.'

Netty was furious: 'I'm just eleven,' she said coldly.

'So am I,' said the other girl.

Netty felt tempted to say 'Liar'; but instead she asked, 'Have you an elder sister?'

'No.'

'What's your name?'

Again that irritating monosyllable. Netty refused to acknowledge it. 'Did you say Jess?' she asked.

'Yes. Jess.'

In spite of what she felt, Netty decided not to argue about that Jess, but went on: 'Jess what?'

The girl looked blank.

'I'm Netty Barr; you're Jess Something – Jess what?'

This time they were getting somewhere: after a tiny hesitation, the girl said, 'Oakes'.

'Jess Oakes. Jessy Oakes.' But whichever way you said it, Netty decided, it didn't sound quite right; and that was because Jess Oakes herself didn't seem quite right. Netty wished now that she weren't sitting next to her.

At playtime Netty went out into the playground; Jess Oakes followed her closely. Netty didn't like that. Unmistakably, Jess Oakes wanted to stick with her. Why? She hadn't wanted to answer Netty's questions; she hadn't been really friendly. But she clung to Netty. Netty didn't like it – didn't like *her*.

Netty managed to shake Jess Oakes off, but then saw her talking with Sid on the other side of the playground. That made her uneasy. But Jess Oakes did not reappear in the classroom after playtime: Netty felt relieved, although she wondered. The teacher made no remark.

Netty went cheerfully home to tea, a little after Sid.

And there was Jess Oakes sitting with Sid in front of the television set. Netty went into the kitchen, to her mother.

'Here you are,' said Mrs Barr. 'You can take all the teas in.' She was loading a tray.

'When did *she* come?' asked Netty.

'With Sid. Sid said she was your friend.' Netty said nothing. 'She's a lot older than you are, Netty.'

'She's exactly my age. So she says.'

'Well, I suppose with that face and that figure – or that no-figure – she could be any age. Any age.'

57

'Yes.'

Mrs Barr looked thoughtfully at Netty, put down the breadknife she still held, and with decision set her hands on her hips: 'Netty!'

'Yes?'

'I don't care what age she is, I like your friends better washed than that.'

Netty gaped at her mother.

'She smells,' said Mrs Barr. 'I don't say it's unwashed body, I don't say it's unwashed clothes – although I don't think much of hers. All I know is she smells nasty.'

'Rotty,' said Netty under her breath.

'Don't bring her again,' said Mrs Barr crisply.

Netty took the tea-tray in to the other two. In the semi-dark they all munched and sipped while they watched the TV serial. But Netty was watching Jess Oakes: the girl only seemed to munch and sip; she ate nothing, drank nothing.

A friend called for Sid, and he went out. Mrs Barr looked in to ask if the girls wanted more tea; Netty said no. When her mother had gone, Netty turned off the television and switched on the light. She faced Jess Oakes: 'What do you want?'

The girl's green glance slid away from Netty. 'No harm. To know something.'

'What?'

'The way home.'

Netty did not ask where she had been living, or why she was lost, or any other commonsense questions. They weren't the right questions, she knew. She just said savagely: 'I wish I knew what was going on inside your head, Jess Oakes.'

Jess Oakes laughed almost aloud, as though Netty had

said something really amusing. She reached out her hand and touched Netty, for the first time: her touch was cool, damp. 'You shall,' she said. 'You shall.'

And where was Netty now? If she were asleep and dreaming, the falling asleep had been very sudden, at the merest touch of a cool, damp hand. But certainly Netty must be dreaming . . .

She dreamt that she was in a strange room filled with a greenish light that seemed partly to come in through two windows, of curious shape, set together rather low down at one side. The walls and ceilings of this chamber were continuous, as in a dome; all curved. There was nothing inside the dome-shaped chamber except the greenish light, of a curious intensity; and Netty. For some reason Netty wanted to look out of the two windows, but she knew that before she could do that, something was required of her. In her dreaming state, she was not at first sure what this was, except that it was tall – very tall – and green. Of course, green: green in spring and summer, and softly singing to itself with leaves; in autumn, yellow and brown and red, and its leaves falling. In winter, leafless. A tree, a forest tree, a tree of the Forest, a tree of Epping Forest. A tree – a hundred trees – a thousand trees – a choice of all the trees of Epping Forest. She had been to the Forest; she was older than Sid, and therefore she knew the direction in which the Forest lay, the direction in which one would have to go to reach the Forest. Her knowledge of the Forest and its whereabouts was in the green-glowing room, and it passed from her in that room, and became someone else's knowledge too . . .

Now Netty knew that she was free to look out of the windows of the room. Their frames were curiously curved;

there was not glass in them, but some other greenish-grey substance. She approached the windows; she looked through them; and she saw into the Barrs' sitting-room, and she saw Netty Barr sitting in her chair by the television set, huddled in sudden sleep.

She saw herself apart from herself, and she cried out in terror, so that she woke, and she was sitting in her chair, and the girl who called herself Jess Oakes was staring at her with her grey-green eyes, smiling.

'Thank you,' said Jess Oakes. 'Now I know all I need to know.' She got up, unmistakably to go. 'Good-bye.'

She went out of the sitting-room, leaving the door open; Netty heard her go out of the front door, leaving that open too. The doors began to bang in a wind that had risen. The front gate banged as well.

Mrs Barr came crossly out of the kitchen to complain. She saw that Netty was alone in the sitting-room. 'Has she gone, then?'

Netty nodded, dumb.

They went into the hall together. Scattered along the hall were pieces of clothing: one gym-shoe by the sitting-room door, another by the coat-hooks; a dingy green dress, looking like something out of a dressing-up box, by the open front door . . .

Mrs Barr ran to the front gate and looked up and down the road. No one; just old Mr Brown on the lookout, as usual. Mrs Barr called to him: 'Have you seen anyone?'

'No. Who should I have seen?'

Mrs Barr came back, shaken. 'She can't have gone stark naked,' she said. Then, as an afterthought, 'She can't have gone, anyway.' Then, again, 'But she has gone.'

Netty was looking at the gym-shoes in the hall. She

could see inside one of them; and she could see a name printed there. It would not be JESS OAKES; it would be some other name. Now she would find out the true identity of the girl with the greenish eyes. She stooped, picked up the shoe, read the name: NETTY BARR.

'Those are the gym-shoes you lost at school,' said Mrs Barr. 'How did she get hold of them? Why was she wearing them? What kind of a girl or a woman was she, with that smell on her? Where did she come from? And where's she gone? Netty, you bad girl, what kind of a friend was she?'

'She wasn't my friend,' said Netty.

'What was she then? And where's she gone – *where's she gone?*'

'I don't know,' said Netty. 'But guess.'

At the River-Gates

LOTS of sisters I had (said the old man), good girls, too; and one elder brother. Just the one. We were at either end of the family: the eldest, my brother John – we always called him Beany, for some reason; then the girls, four of them; then me. I was Tiddler, and the reason for that was plain.

Our father was a flour miller, and we lived just beside the mill. It was a water-mill, built right over the river, with the mill-wheel underneath. To understand what happened that wild night, all those years ago, you have to understand a bit about the working of the mill-stream. About a hundred yards before the river reached the mill, it divided: the upper river flowed on to power the mill, as I've said; the lower river, leaving the upper river through sluice-gates, flowed to one side of the mill and past it; and then the upper and lower rivers joined up again well below the mill. The sluice-gates could be opened or shut by the miller to let more or less water through from the upper to the lower river. You can see the use of that: the miller controlled the flow of water to power his mill; he could also draw off any floodwaters that came down.

Being a miller's son, I can never remember not under-standing that. I was a little tiddler, still at school, when my brother, Beany, began helping my father in the mill. He was as good as a man, my father said. He was strong, and he learnt the feel of the grain, and he was clever with the mill

machinery, and he got on with the other men in the mill –
there were only ten of them, counting two carters. He
understood the gates, of course, and how to get just the
right head of water for the mill. And he liked it all: he liked
the work he did, and the life; he liked the mill, and the river,
and the long river-bank. One day he'd be the miller after
my father, everyone said.

I was too young to feel jealousy about that; but I would
never have felt jealous of Beany, because Beany was the
best brother you could have had. I loved and admired him
more than anyone I knew or could imagine knowing. He
was very good to me. He used to take me with him when
you might have thought a little boy would have been in the
way. He took me with him when he went fishing, and he
taught me to fish. I learnt patience, then, from Beany.
There were plenty of roach and dace in the river; and
sometimes we caught trout or pike; and once we caught an
eel, and I was first of all terrified and then screaming with
excitement at the way it whipped about on the bank, but
Beany held it and killed it, and my mother made it into eel-
pie. He knew about the fish in the river, and the little
creatures, too. He showed me fresh-water shrimps, and
leeches – 'Look, Tiddler, they make themselves into
croquet-hoops when they want to go anywhere!' and he
showed me the little underwater cottages of caddis-worms.
He knew where to get good watercress for Sunday tea – you
could eat watercress from our river, in those days.

We had an old boat on the river, and Beany would take it
upstream to inspect the banks for my father. The banks
had to be kept sound: if there was a breach, it would let the
water escape and reduce the water-power for the mill.
Beany took Jess, our dog, with him in the boat, and he often

took me. Beany was the only person I've ever known who could point out a kingfisher's nest in the river-bank. He knew about birds. He once showed me a flycatcher's nest in the brickwork below the sluice-gates, just above where the water dashed and roared at its highest. Once, when we were in the boat, he pointed ahead to an otter in the water. I held on to Jess's collar then.

It was Beany who taught me to swim. One summer it was hotter than anyone remembered, and Beany was going from the mill up to the gates to shut in more water. Jess was following him, and as he went he gave me a wink, so I followed too, although I didn't know why. As usual, he opened the gates with the great iron spanner, almost as long in the handle as he was tall. Then he went down to the pool in the lower river, as if to see the water-level there. But as he went he was unbuttoning his flour-whitened waistcoat; by the time he reached the pool he was naked, and he dived straight in. He came up with his hair plastered over his eyes, and he called to me: 'Come on, Tiddler! Just time for a swimming lesson!' Jess sat on the bank and watched us.

Jess was really my father's dog, but she attached herself to Beany. She loved Beany. Everyone loved Beany, and he was good to everyone. Especially, as I've said, to me. Just sometimes he'd say, 'I'm off on my own now, Tiddler,' and then I knew better than to ask to go with him. He'd go sauntering up the river-bank by himself, except for Jess at his heels. I don't think he did anything very particular when he went off on his own. Just the river and the river-bank were happiness enough for him.

He was still not old enough to have got himself a girl, which might have changed things a bit; but he wasn't too young to go to the War. The War broke out in 1914, when I was still a boy, and Beany went.

It was sad without Beany; but it was worse than that. I was too young to understand then; but, looking back, I realize what was wrong. There was fear in the house. My parents became gloomy and somehow secret. So many young men were being killed at the Front. Other families in the village had had word of a son's death. The news came in a telegram. I overheard my parents talking of those deaths, those telegrams, although not in front of the girls or me. I saw my mother once, in the middle of the morning, kneeling by Beany's bed, praying.

So every time Beany came home on leave, alive, we were lucky.

But when Beany came, he was different. He loved us as much, but he was different. He didn't play with me as he used to do; he would sometimes stare at me as though he didn't see me. When I shouted 'Beany!' and rushed at him, he would start as if he'd woken up. Then he'd smile, and be good to me, almost as he used to be. But, more often than he used to, he'd be off all by himself up the river-bank, with Jess at his heels. My mother, who longed to have him within her sight for every minute of his leave, used to watch him go, and sigh. Once I heard her say to my father that the river-bank did Beany good, as if he were sickening for some strange disease. Once one of the girls was asking Beany about the Front and the trenches, and he was telling her this and that, and we were all interested, and suddenly he stopped and said, 'No. It's hell.' And walked away alone, up the green, quiet river-bank. I suppose if one place was hell, then the other was heaven to him.

After Beany's leaves were over, the mill-house was

gloomy again; and my father had to work harder, without Beany's help in the mill. Nowadays he had to work the gates all by himself, a thing that Beany had been taking over from him. If the gates needed working at night, my father and Beany had always gone there together. My mother hated it nowadays when my father had to go to the gates alone at night: she was afraid he'd slip and fall in the water, and, although he could swim, accidents could happen to a man alone in the dark. But, of course, my father wouldn't let her come with him, or any of my sisters, and I was still considered much too young. That irked me.

Well, one season had been very dry and the river level had dropped. The gates were kept shut to get up a head of water for the mill. Then clouds began to build up heavily on the horizon, and my father said he was sure it was going to rain; but it didn't. All day storms rumbled in the distance. In the evening the rain began. It rained steadily: my father had already been once to the gates to open the flashes. He was back at home, drying off in front of the fire. The rain still drove against the windows. My mother said, 'It can't come down worse than this.' She and my sisters were still up with my father. Even I wasn't in bed, although I was supposed to have been. No one could have slept for the noise of the rain.

Suddenly the storm grew worse – much worse. It seemed to explode over our heads. We heard a pane of glass in the skylight over the stairs shatter with the force of it, and my sisters ran with buckets to catch the water pouring through. Oddly, my mother didn't go to see the damage: she stayed with my father, watching him like a lynx. He was fidgeting up and down, paying no attention to the skylight either, and suddenly he said he'd have to go up to the gates again and open everything to carry all possible floodwater into the lower river. This was what my mother had been dreading. She made a great outcry, but she knew it was no use. My father put on his tarpaulin jacket again and took his oil lamp and a thick stick – I don't know why, nor did he, I think. Jess always hated being out in the rain, but she followed him. My mother watched him from the back door, lamenting, and urging him to be careful. A few steps from the doorway and you couldn't see him any longer for the driving rain.

My mother's lingering at the back door gave me my

chance. I got my boots on and an oilskin cape I had (I wasn't a fool, even if I was little) and I whipped out of the front door and worked my way round in the shelter of the house to the back and then took the path my father had taken to the river, and made a dash for it, and caught up with my father and Jess, just as they were turning up the way towards the gates. I held on to Jess's tail for quite a bit before my father noticed me. He was terribly angry, of course, but he didn't want to turn back with me, and he didn't like to send me back alone, and perhaps in his heart of hearts he was glad of a little human company on such a night. So we all three struggled up to the gates together. Just by the gates my father found me some shelter between a tree-trunk and a stack of drift-wood. There I crouched, with Jess to keep me company.

I was too small to help my father with the gates, but there was one thing I could do. He told me to hold his lamp so that the light shone on the gates and what he was doing. The illumination was very poor, partly because of the driving rain, but at least it was better than nothing, and anyway my father knew those gates by heart. Perhaps he gave me the job of holding the light so that I had something to occupy my mind and keep me from being afraid.

There was plenty to be afraid of on that night of storm.

Directing what light I could on to my father also directed and concentrated my attention on him. I could see his laborious motions as he heaved the great spanner into place. Then he began to try to rack up with it, but the wind and the rain were so strong that I could see he was having the greatest difficulty. Once I saw him stagger sideways nearly into the blackness of the river. Then I wanted to run out from my shelter and try to help him, but he had strictly

68

forbidden me to do any such thing, and I knew he was right.

Young as I was, I knew – it came to me as I watched him – that he couldn't manage the gates alone in that storm. I suppose he was a man already just past the prime of his strength: the wind and the rain were beating him; the river would beat him.

I shone the light as steadily as I could, and gripped Jess by the collar, and I think I prayed.

I was so frightened then that, afterwards, when I wasn't frightened, I could never be sure of what I had seen, or what I thought I had seen, or what I imagined I had seen. Through the confusion of the storm I saw my father struggling and staggering, and, as I peered and peered, my vision seemed to blur and to double, so that I began sometimes to see one man, sometimes two. My father seemed to have a shadow-self besides himself, who steadied him, heaved with him, worked with him, and at last together they had opened the sluice-gates and let the flood through.

When it was done, my father came back to where Jess and I were, and leant against the tree. He was gasping for breath and exhausted, and had a look on his face that I cannot describe. From his expression I knew that he had *felt* the shadow with him, just as I had seen it. And Jess was agitated too, straining against my hold, whining.

I looked past my father, and I could still see something by the sluice-gates: a shadow that had separated itself from my father, and lingered there. I don't know how I could have seen it in the darkness. I don't know. My father slowly turned and looked in the direction that he saw me looking. The shadow began to move away from the gates, away from

us; it began to go up the long river-bank beyond the gates, into the darkness there. It seemed to me that the rain and the wind stilled a little as it went.

Jess wriggled from my grasp and was across the gates and up the river-bank, following the vanished shadow. I had made no move, uttered no word, but my father said to me, 'Let them go!' I looked up at him, and his face was streaming with tears as well as with rain.

He took my hand and we fought our way back to the house. The whole house was lit up, to light us home, and my mother stood at the back door, waiting. She gave a cry of horror when she saw me with my father; and then she saw his face, and her own went quite white. He stumbled into her arms, and he sobbed and sobbed. I didn't know until that night that grown men could cry. My mother led my father indoors, and I don't know what talk they had together. My sisters looked after me, dried me, scolded me, put me to bed.

The next day the telegram came to say that Beany had been killed in action in Flanders.

It was some time after that that Jess came home. She was wet through, and my mother thought she was ill, for she sat shivering by the fire, and for two days would neither eat nor drink. My father said: 'Let her be.'

I'm an old man: it all happened so many years ago, but I've never forgotten my brother Beany. He was so good to us all.

Her Father's Attic

ROSAMUND was an only child, and the apple of her mother's eye. She resembled her mother: pink cheeked, golden haired, blue eyed. She was going to be like her mother: pretty.

Mrs Brunning had faith in her daughter's looks. 'She'll be picked out,' she said. 'She'll go up to London and be a model. Or go on telly. She'll make a name for herself, and money; and marry well . . . What did you say, Geoff?'

But Mr Brunning, who was hungry from working out of doors, had only grunted: his attention was entirely on his dinner. Besides, he knew the kind of thing that would come next.

'Anyway,' his wife said, 'she won't hang about here until some drudging clodhopper marries her, and she has to end her days where she began 'em.'

This was a dig at her husband, who was a small farmer and an unsuccessful one: he worked hard on his land for very little return. He had inherited his father's farm and farmhouse only because none of his four elder brothers had wanted to: they had had higher ambitions, and achieved them. He had been the runt of the family, small, sallow, timid; he had been teased and persecuted all his childhood. He had married – so his wife considered – above him; and he would be teased and persecuted for the rest of his married life.

'Rosamund has more of me in her than she has of you,

thank goodness,' said Mrs Brunning. 'She's all me, is Rosamund.'

Rosamund, above whose head her mother wrangled, yawned inside her mouth and was glad that dinner was over. Her father got up and went back to his work outside, and Mrs Brunning began washing up. There was no question of Rosamund's helping: she was the only child, spoilt, her mother's darling. Mrs Brunning considered most of the local children unfit company for her; so, as often before, Rosamund went off now to play alone indoors. Indoors, because her mother hated farm-filth, as she called it, ever to be on her feet.

Brunning's was an old house, although without any particular history – Geoffrey Brunning could say only that his father knew that *his* father had been born there. It was not at all a grand house, but it had been built for a time of many children and of farm-servants living with their masters. Nowadays there were shut rooms and unused passageways, away from the central, lived-in part of the house; such outlying parts suffered the erosions of neglect and time. Since Geoffrey Brunning's childhood, for instance, the highest attic, once a nursery, had been closed. Mr Brunning said the floor was unsafe, and – particularly to safeguard Rosamund – had locked the door that opened to the attic stairway.

So the door was already locked before Rosamund was old enough to roam the house on her own, and soon after that the woodworm had begun their invisible banquet upon the framework. Rosamund used regularly to bang at the closed door as she passed it, but without real curiosity. Perhaps her knock interrupted the woodworms' gnawing for a moment; then they resumed. Neither she nor they, after the passage of years, were at all prepared for the day – this very day – when their world exploded in a flurry of wood-dust, as her casual blow sent the metalwork of the lock right through the decayed woodwork of the frame. Abruptly the door swung open as if to open wide, then its hinges creaked to a rusty standstill, and Rosamund was left with a sliced-off view of wooden stairs powdered with old plaster and new wood-dust.

Of course, Rosamund had always known of the existence of the attic, but the opening of the way to it was new. She must – she *must* go up and see it for herself. Circumstances were favourable: her father was out on the farm; her mother would still be in the kitchen, either finishing washing up or beginning to prepare for a genteel visitor that afternoon. Between the kitchen and the attic lay a wasteland of empty rooms and passages. Rosamund listened carefully, but she could hear no sound from anywhere.

She took a deeper breath than usual, and pushed firmly against the door. It offered surprising resistance, but finally opened wide enough to allow her body to pass through. She began going carefully up into the darkness of the stairway, feeling before her with her hands.

At the top of the stairs, she stubbed her fingers against another door. It had a small round hole at the level of a handle, but a spider had been at work and her peeping eye could see only a mesh illumined from beyond by a dim lemon-coloured light.

For the first time, with darkness round her, and the unbroken silence of years, she nearly felt afraid, but would not allow the feeling to grow upon her. She pressed very softly at the door. At once, with a kind of over-eagerness, the door swung right back.

74

She stood on the threshold of her father's attic-nursery. Its bare length stretched uninterruptedly from her feet to a small window at the far end, where the afternoon sunlight shone weakly through dusty glass, greenish yellow where the last leaves of a creeper encroached upon the panes.

She was not afraid now. Being a practical child, she first considered the floor, which her father had said was unsafe. The bare boards looked firm, and she began to test them, one after another. They bore her weight. She knew that she was not as heavy as a grown up person, yet she felt beneath her feet the solid assurance of timber that would outlast generations. The floor was sound, when her father had said it was not: she felt puzzled.

There was no other mystery to the room. It was quite empty, except for the low shelves and cupboards that had been built into the steep angle where the sloping roof met the floor. She examined the cupboards carefully: they were all quite empty, even the one with the door that appeared to be locked but was only jammed. Someone, at some time, had forced the door, and damaged it. Delicately she eased it open. She left that door standing ajar, because it had been so difficult. She might want to get in again. The cupboard was a roomy one, without shelves.

Rosamund went to the window next. With the stubbornness of disuse, it refused to open; but she cleared a pane of glass and could look through. She was charmed with the novelty of the view from here. She looked right across the roofs of the farm-buildings to the fields and the spire of the parish church beyond. She thought that she could distinguish her father at work in one of the middle fields, but the light was failing. The setting sun stood in irregular red slices behind a thin copse of trees on the skyline.

Having gazed for so long into the last of the sun, she was surprised at the darkness of the room when she turned back to it. Shadows had gathered thickly at the far end, by the door; and inky blackness had settled in the depth of the one cupboard left open. She decided suddenly that it was time to leave the attic.

She started off across the safe, safe floor towards the stairway that led back to the peopled part of the house.

The attic was a long one and Rosamund walked slowly, because still with that careful, light step – she could not quite put from her mind the idea that the place was dangerous. She drew level with the open cupboard, and looked deeply into it. She halted as it occurred to her – without surprise or pleasure – that this cupboard would make a good hiding-place: it was large enough for a child of her age, crouching. Neither excitement nor pleasure; neither surprise nor speculation – she seemed to have remembered the possibilities of the cupboard, rather than freshly to have thought of them.

There she stood, staring into the cupboard.

The sun had gone, and the shadows of the room moved up towards the window. They lapped round Rosamund like a sea, and she began to sink into them like a drowning person. She sank to the floor and lay along it, quite still. Her eyes were wide open, fixed upon the darkness in the cupboard. Darkness and fear flowed from the cupboard and filled the attic from doorway to window.

Outside in the field Geoffrey Brunning was still working in the afterlight. Now he stopped abruptly: he told himself he had forgotten that he must go in early today. He must go.

He had forgotten nothing; but it was as if something had remembered *him*. He did not know why he was going – why he was hurrying. As he neared the farmhouse he broke into an awkward, anxious trot.

He went in by the back door as usual, leaving his boots there, and so into the kitchen. It was empty and almost dark except for the red glow from the old-fashioned stove that his wife was always complaining about.

'Ros!' he called. There was no answer.

He decided to have some commonsense. He switched on the light, filled the kettle and put it on to boil, and began to cut bread for toast. He cut one slice, then laid the knife carefully down and went to stand out in the hall. It was dark there, with only a line of light from underneath the door of the sitting-room. That was where his wife would be entertaining. He could hear voices, but not Rosamund's. He had not expected to hear it.

He turned away from the door of the sitting-room, as he had turned away from the kitchen; and now he faced the main stairs. In the dark he could hardly see them. He stood peering, trying to make his mind work commonsensically; to think of the electric light switch that would banish darkness. But darkness increased moment by moment, filling his mind. Darkness and fear flowed round him like a sea, rose round him to drown him.

He gave a cry and turned quickly back to the light of the kitchen. Then, at the very door, he swerved aside and set off at a rush, but not firmly; stumbling and feeling like a blind man up the stairs, along walls, round corners. His course was directly up and towards the disused attic.

At the threshold of the attic he took a deep breath, like a man about to enter a smoke-filled room. He could see nothing, but he knew that Rosamund was there. He made one mistake, in thinking – in being sure – that she would be crouching in the cupboard with the jammed door. Even as his feet felt their way towards it, they met her body on the floor. He bent, took hold of her, and dragged her to the top of the attic stairway; then, having gathered her in his arms, he carried her down and away, to the kitchen. There he set

her upon a chair, where she began to stir and blink in the bright light, like a dreamer waking; but she had not been asleep. She was very pale at first, but soon the pink began to reappear in her cheeks. She did not speak to her father, but her awakened gaze never left him.

Her father had collapsed upon another chair in the kitchen.

There Mrs Brunning found them, having said good-bye to her visitor. Her daughter seemed as usual, but her hus-

band was leaning forward in an attitude of exhaustion, his fingers dangling over the edge of his knees, his face white and sweaty.

'Don't say you're sickening for something, now!' Mrs Brunning said sharply. 'You're a sight! What do you feel like?'

'Oh . . . I feel . . .'

What did he feel like?

Long ago, when he was a child, he had felt like this, once. His brothers had shut him into one of the nursery cupboards, just for their fun; and the cupboard door had jammed. That was all it had been, except for the darkness inside the cupboard; and his fear. The darkness and the fear had lasted forever. They said afterwards that his being shut in had all lasted only a short time, and that he had been stupid to be so afraid. They'd been able to force the cupboard door open in the end, and then they'd dragged him out. But the darkness had stayed behind in the cupboard; and his fear.

'Well, what do you feel like?' his wife repeated irritably.

'Nothing special.'

'Let's hope you pass nothing special on to Rosamund, then. But at least she's not one of those easy-ailing children. Like me, in that.'

Rosamund was staring at her father, paying no attention to her mother's refrain: 'Yes, more of me in her than you, thank goodness. All me.' Rosamund was staring at her father as at somebody strange to her, and of the strangest importance.

The Running-Companion

ANY day, over the great expanses of the Common, you can see runners. In track-suits or shorts and running-tops, they trot along the asphalted paths across the grass, or among the trees, or by the Ponds. On the whole, they avoid London Hill, towards the middle of the Common, because of its steepness. There is another reason. People climb the Hill for the magnificence of the view of London from the top; but runners consider it unlucky, especially at dusk. They say it is haunted by ghosts and horrors then. One ghost; one horror.

In his lifetime, Mr Kenneth Adamson was one of the daily runners. This was a good many years ago now. His story has been pieced together from what was reported in the newspapers, what was remembered by neighbours and eye-witnesses, and what may have been supposed to have been going on in the mind of Mr Adamson himself.

Sometimes Mr Adamson ran on the Common in the early morning; more often he ran in the evening after work. He worked in an office. He was not liked there: he was silent, secretive, severe. People were afraid of him.

The Adamsons lived in one of the terrace-houses bordering the Common. There was old Mrs Adamson, a widow, who hardly comes into this story at all; and her two sons, of whom Kenneth, or Ken, was the elder. There were only two people in the world who called Mr Adamson by his first name: they were his mother and his brother. He had no wife or girl-friend; no friends at all.

Mr Adamson ran daily in order to keep himself fit. The steady jog-trot of this kind of running soothed his whole being; even his mind was soothed. While his legs ran a familiar track, his mind ran along an equally familiar one. Ran, and then ran back, and then ran on again: his mind covered the same ground over and over and over again.

His mind ran on his hatred.

Mr Adamson's hatred was so well grown and in such constant training that at times it seemed to him like another living being. In his mind there were the three of them: himself; and his hatred; and his brother, the object of his hatred.

Of course, Mr Adamson's brother never ran. He could not walk properly without a crutch; he could only just manage to get upstairs and downstairs by himself in their own house. He had been crippled in early childhood, in an accident; and his mother had not only cared for him, but spoilt him. To Mr Adamson's way of thinking, she had neglected *him*. Jealousy had been the beginning of Mr Adamson's hatred, in childhood: as the jealousy grew, the hatred grew, like a poison tree in his mind. It grew all the more strongly because Mr Adamson had always kept quiet about it: he kept his hatred quiet inside his mind.

He grew up; and his hatred grew up with him.

For years now Mr Adamson's hatred had been with him, not only when he ran, but all day, and often at night, too. Sometimes in his dreams it seemed to him that his running-companion, his hatred, stood just behind him, or at his very elbow, a person. By turning his head he would be able to see that person. He knew that his hatred was full-grown now; and he longed to know what it looked like. Was it monster or man? Had it a heavy body, like his own, to labour uphill only with effort; or had it a real runner's physique, lean and leggy? He had only to turn his head and see; but in his dreams he was always prevented.

'Ken!'

His mother's thin old voice, calling his name up the stairs, would break into his dreams, summoning him down to breakfast. Mr Adamson breakfasted alone, listening to the sound of his brother moving about in his room above, or perhaps beginning his slow, careful descent of the stairs. Listening to that, it seemed to Mr Adamson that he heard something else: a friend's voice at his ear, whispering a promise: 'One day, Ken . . .'

One day, at last, Mrs Adamson died of old age. The two brothers were left alone together in the house on the edge of the Common. They would have to manage, people said. On the morning after the funeral, Mr Adamson prepared the day's meals, then went off to his office. At this time of year, he ran in the evenings, never in the mornings. It was the beginning of autumn and still pleasant on the Common in the evening, in spite of mist.

Mr Adamson came home from work; and presumably the two brothers had supper, talked perhaps – although Mr Adamson never spoke to his brother if he could help it – and prepared for bed. Just before bedtime, as usual, Mr Adamson must have changed into his running shorts and top and training shoes and set off on his evening run.

Questioned afterwards, the neighbours said that the evening seemed no different from any other evening. But how were they to know? The Adamsons lived in a house whose party-walls let little noise through. Would they have heard a cry of fear: 'Ken – no!' Would they have heard a scream? The sound of a heavy body falling – falling –?

Some time that evening Mr Adamson's brother fell downstairs, fatally, from the top of the stairs to the bottom. Whether he fell by his own mischance (but no, in all his life, he had never had an accident on those stairs), or whether he was pushed – nothing was ever officially admitted. But the evidence examined afterwards at least pointed to his already lying there at the foot of the stairs, huddled, still, when Mr Adamson went out for his evening run. Mr Adamson must have had to step over his dead body as he came downstairs, in his running gear, to go out on the Common.

It so happened that neighbours did see Mr Adamson leaving the house. He left it looking as usual – or almost as usual, they said. One neighbour remarked that Mr Adamson seemed to be smiling. He never smiled, normally. They saw no one come out of the house with him, of course. No one followed him.

Mr Adamson set off across the Common, as usual increasing his pace until it reached a jog-trot. This was the speed that suited him. Joints loosened; heartbeats and breathing steadied; the air was on his face; only the sky above him. His mind felt both satisfied and empty: free. This was going to be the run of his life.

He planned to run across the Common to the Ponds; then take the main exit route from the Common, leading to the bus terminus and shopping centre; but he would veer away just before reaching them, taking a side path that circled the base of London Hill; and so home.

When he got home, he would ring the doctor or the police, or both, to report his brother's accident. He had no fear of the police. No fear of anyone.

Now, as he ran, he began to get his second wind, and to

feel that he could run forever. No, the police would never catch up with him. No one could ever catch up with him.

Pleasantly he ran as far as the Ponds, whose shores were deserted even of ducks. Mist was rising from the water, as dusk descended from the sky. Mr Adamson wheeled round by the Ponds and took the path towards the terminus and shopping centre. He was running well; it seemed to him, superbly.

A runner going well is seldom aware of the sound of his own footfalls, even on an asphalted surface. But Mr Adamson began to notice an odd, distant echo of his own footsteps: perhaps, he thought, an effect of the mist, or of the nearness of London Hill.

Running, he listened to the echo. Unmistakably, running footsteps in the distance: a most curious effect.

Running, listening carefully, he began to change his mind. Those distant footsteps were neither his own nor an echo of his own, after all. Someone behind him was running in the same direction as himself, trotting so exactly at his own pace that he had been deceived into supposing echoes. The footsteps were not so very far in the distance, either. Although the pace was so exactly his own, yet the footsteps of the other runner seemed all the time to be coming a little nearer. The impossibility of this being so made Mr Adamson want to laugh, for the first time in many years. But you don't laugh as you run.

Very slightly Mr Adamson increased the pace of his running, and maintained it; and listened. The runner behind seemed also to have very slightly increased his pace: the footsteps were a little more rapid, surely, and clearer. Clearer? *Nearer?* Mr Adamson had intended to leave the main way across the Common only just before it reached the terminus and shops: now he decided to take a side path at once. It occurred to him that the runner might just be someone hurrying to catch a bus from the terminus. That supposition was a relief.

He turned along the side path; and the feet behind, in due time, turned too. They began to follow Mr Adamson along the side path, never losing ground, very slightly gaining it.

Mr Adamson quickened his pace yet again: he was now running faster than he liked. He decided to double back to the main path, across the grass.

The grass was soft and silent under his feet. He heard nothing of his own footfalls; he heard no footfalls behind him. Now he was on the main path again, and still could hear nothing behind him. Thankfully he prepared to slacken his pace.

Then he heard them. The runner behind him must have crossed the soundless grass at a different angle from his own. The strange runner's feet now struck the asphalt of the path behind Mr Adamson nearer than he could possibly have expected – much nearer.

The pace was still the same as his own, yet gained upon him very slightly all the time. He had no inclination to laugh now. He ran faster – faster. The sweat broke on him, ran into his eyes, almost blinding him.

He reached his intended turning off the main path and took it. The feet, in due time, followed him. Too late he wished that he had continued on the main path right to the bus terminus and the shops, to the bright lights of streets and buses and shops. But now he had turned back over the Common, duskier and mistier than ever. He had before him the long path winding round the base of London Hill before it took him home. It was a long way, and a lonely, unfrequented one at this time of evening. The Hill was straight ahead of him, and he knew there would be groups of people at the top, people who walked there in the evening to admire the view. Never before had he chosen to go where there were other human beings, just because they were other human beings, flesh and blood like himself. Now he did. He took the path that led directly to the summit of the Hill.

The evening strollers on the top of the Hill had been looking at the view, and one or two had begun to watch the runner on the slopes below. He was behaving oddly. They had watched him change course, and then double to and fro – 'like a rabbit with something after it', as one watcher said.

'He's coming this way,' said another.

'Straight up the Hill,' observed someone else in the little crowd. Most of them were now peering down through the dusk. 'Straight up the Hill – you need to be young and really in training for that.'

Straight up the Hill he went, his heart hammering against his ribs, his breath tearing in and out of his throat, his whole body dripping with sweat. He ran and ran, and behind him came the feet, gaining on him.

On the Hill, they were all staring now at the runner. 'What's got into him?' someone asked. 'You might think all the devils in hell were after him.'

'He'll kill himself with running,' said a young woman. But she was wrong.

Now he was labouring heavily up the steepest part of the slope, almost exhausted. He hardly ran; rather, staggered. Behind him the feet kept their own pace; they did not slow, as his had done. They would catch up with him soon.

Very soon now.

He knew from the loudness of the following feet that the other runner was at his back. He had only to turn his head and he would see him face to face; but that he would not do – that he would never do, to save his very soul.

The footsteps were upon him; a voice close in his ear whispered softly – oh! so softly! – and lovingly – oh! so lovingly! 'Ken!' it whispered, and would not be denied.

The watchers on the Hill peered down.

'Why has he stopped?'

'Why's he turning round?'

'What's he – Oh, my God!'

For Mr Adamson had turned, and seen what none of the watchers on the Hill could see, and he gave a shriek that carried far over the Common and lost itself in darkness and distance – a long, long shriek that will never be forgotten by any that heard it.

He fell where he stood, in a twisted heap.

When they reached him, he was dead. Overstrain of the heart, the doctor said later; but, being a wise man, he offered no explanation of the expression on Mr Adamson's face. There was horror there and – yes, something like dreadful recognition.

All this happened a good many years ago now; but runners on the Common still avoid London Hill, because of Mr Adamson and whatever came behind him. There may be some runners who fear on their own account – fear the footsteps that might follow *them*, fear to turn and see the face of their own dearest, worst wickedness. Let us hope not.

Beckoned

FAWCETT'S, as the house was called, stood alone. It was not very much older nor very much larger than the pink-bricked houses that surrounded it in their rows and courts and crescents; but the unkemptness of its garden and its own dark desolate aspect set it apart. No one lived there but old Mr Fawcett, a widower, ailing. No one used its weedy front drive but the District Nurse and Mrs Pugh (who had cleaned and shopped and cooked for Mr Fawcett for years) and the occasional baffled hawker. Mr Fawcett never went out: never.

The play-space for the children of the housing-estate extended to Fawcett's boundary, marked by a grim old brick wall, now broken or breaking in several places, but a formidable barrier still. Of the children of the estate, Peter was the one who went over oftenest, because he was the best at finding old tennis balls or footballs. He had a knack. He didn't mind looking for a lost ball, which most people hated doing, because of his special trick; but he didn't much like Fawcett's.

'Go on, Peter!' they said. 'Find it for us!' And gave him a leg up over the wall.

Once over, Peter stood absolutely still among the brambles and the nettles. The voices on the other side of the wall had become indistinct to him, seemed unimportant. He let the playground and the game and the other children drift out of his mind. His mind emptied itself. All that was left was an intentness upon finding a certain old tennis ball.

Then, as always before, he began to move towards the ball. He dodged under a half-fallen tree; he circumnavigated a huge bramble bush; he had his eyes fixed now on a tangle of grass where the ball must be, when he was interrupted.

Something interfered with his reception of the message of the ball's whereabouts; something deflected his course. He hesitated, stopped; then turned aside and began to move along what, from the feel of the ground under his feet, might once have been a gravelled path. The path took him through garden-jungle until he found himself facing the back of Fawcett's itself, across the weedy rankness of a neglected lawn. He saw the house as a whole, almost black against the winter sunset. The windows were all blank and unlit, except for a weak glow from one upper room. But his attention focused on the ground floor and on the french windows that opened – if they could ever be forced over the weeds just outside – onto a little paved terrace. He became aware of a slight movement and a variation of darkness on the other side of the french windows. He realized that he was looking at someone on the other side of the glass – someone who was almost certainly looking at him. Whoever it was moved close up to the window, and thereby became more distinct. He saw the tallness of a human figure, wrapped in some long dark-striped garment, presumably a dressing-gown; he saw the pallor of face and hands, and the movement of the hands: one hand moved to the middle of the window, where the catch would be; the other hand was raised in a gesture which Peter guessed rather than clearly saw. The figure beckoned to him.

Peter knew that he was trespassing; but perhaps that was not all that frightened him. He felt his skin sweating, warm for an instant, then cold. The chill made him shiver, and the shiver set him free. Suddenly his mind was empty no longer: he was thinking of his own fear, and of his trespassing, and of the boys waiting in the playground, and of his own fear again.

He slewed round and rushed back the way he had come, to the wall and over it, into the playground again.

'Where's the ball?' they cried, crowding round him.

'I couldn't find it.'

'You always find it! Why couldn't you find it? We haven't another. Go back, Peter. Find it. You always find it. Go back.'

'No,' said Peter. 'I shan't. I'm going home.' He set off at a run, with the others jeering at him, saying they would go over in a body to find the ball.

In the end, none of them went, either singly or in a group. No one quite liked going into Fawcett's after dark, and it was gloaming already.

When Peter reached home, he did not speak of his experience at Fawcett's, partly because he knew his parents would be sharp with him about his trespassing right up to the house – especially as he had been caught at it; partly, too, because the incident had been unimportant; and partly for the exactly opposite reason – that it had been important *to him*. He tried to recall what little he knew of Fawcett's: that the Fawcetts had always lived there, but old Mr Fawcett was the last of them; he had once had a wife, but she had died, not so very long ago; he had once had a son, but he had died as a boy, and that had been a very long time ago indeed. And had there been a daughter too?

'Yes,' said Peter's mother, talking through the whisper of television and the sputter of fat in the pan. 'Yes. A daughter – oh, yes. A good girl; but her father was one of these girls-are-worth-nothing men.' Peter's mother tutted, and it was not because of hot fat spitting out on to her hand. 'He cared nothing for her. Then the boy was born. He was the apple of his father's eye, of course. When he was killed – it was a car-accident, I think – old Mr Fawcett went nearly out of his mind. According to Mrs Pugh, who's always helped there, he went around shouting that the wrong child had died. After that, he couldn't bear to have the daughter about the house. In the end, she had to go. She was just eighteen. A good girl – very like her mother, in some ways. I remember her mother well.'

'I don't remember any of them,' said Peter.

'You weren't born; or too young to notice. The girl went to a job away, and then she married, and had children, and then her husband died. She must have had a hard life. She never came back; she was never allowed back, even after her mother died. She could be keeping house now for her invalid father and making a proper home for her children; but no! Mrs Pugh still does it, stone deaf and one foot in the grave by now.'

'What was the boy like?'

'Just a boy. He was about your age when he died. Your sort of boy, well grown, up to any mischief.' Peter's mother eyed him sardonically. 'I notice you don't ask about Mrs Fawcett.'

'Mrs Fawcett?'

'I suppose you're one of those women-are-worth-nothing people. But Mrs Fawcett was really worth ten of Mr Fawcett, in spite of his loud-mouthed cantankerousness and the fuss he made about getting his own way. Mrs Fawcett was one of those quiet, big women – she was as tall as her husband. Quiet. Patient. Clever. Yes –' Peter's mother had surprised herself by her own conclusion. 'Yes, she was a clever woman, I think. If she'd lived, she'd have got her daughter home again, by hook or by crook, in spite of that brute of a husband.' She began dishing up the supper, having finished all she had to say.

But Peter's father, who had been drowsing in front of the television set, now entered the conversation. 'And if she was so clever, and he was such a brute, why didn't she leave him?'

'Because some women are saints; and she still loved him.' And Peter's mother triumphantly dashed a plate of fish and chips on to her husband's knees. He accepted it, and defeat, together.

Peter went on thinking about Fawcett's, and old Mr Fawcett prowling downstairs in his dressing-gown. He made an excuse to himself to go back: he really must recover that tennis ball. He chose a time early in the morning, when nobody was about, to nip over the wall. There was no need to use his trick of mind-emptying: he knew already where the ball was. He made his way to it, found it, and stood with it in his hand, irresolute. He would have liked to have gone on to the house, as he had done before; but – yes, he was frightened of that. In the end, he climbed back over the wall with his tennis ball.

When he was back outside Fawcett's again, he discovered that he felt disappointed; flat. Also somehow guilty, as though he had left something undone; as though he had failed someone.

So the next day he went again, very early, before school,

with the deliberate intention of going far enough to see the back of the house.

By morning light the house looked less forbidding, but more obviously neglected: there was, of course, not even a light from the upstairs window.

Yet Peter saw that Mr Fawcett was already up and about: from the deep shadows on the other side of the glass of the french windows the same tall figure in the dark striped dressing-gown moved into view. There were the same gestures of opening the windows, of beckoning.

Peter's earlier fears, and any remembrance of his parents' warnings against the acceptance of strange invitations – all vanished. He obeyed the summons. As he crossed the roughness that had once been lawn, the figure behind the glass began to withdraw into the shadows of the interior, still beckoning.

Peter reached the french windows. He had expected to find them ajar for him, but they were not. Perhaps they had been left unlatched, but not open. Sure of this, he pulled hard at them; but something resisted. Perhaps the resistance was from the tough grass clumps that sprang in the pavement crevices outside the windows and grew thickly against the frame and glass. He tugged harder, his mind set upon following where he had been beckoned; something gave sharply, and the windows opened to admit him.

By now the room inside – a dank, gloomy dining-room – was empty: Peter did not doubt that old Mr Fawcett had gone from it to lead the way he was to follow; and certainly the door at the other end of the dining-room stood persuasively open. He followed into the hall. Here he was taken aback, for the various doors round the hall were shut, and surely, if he had been meant to follow, a way would have been left open to him. Then he realized that the stairs lay open to him. He mounted them, and, even before he reached the top, he could see another door open – to a bedroom he supposed.

There were several doors from this upstairs landing, but there was only one open, inviting him. He went in.

Instantly he was aware that this must be the room that he had noticed on the first evening, because of its lighted window. Then, the artificial light from inside had been dim; now the daylight from outside was largely cut off by half-drawn, heavy curtains. But even by the half-light he could see that the room was old Mr Fawcett's, because there was old Mr Fawcett himself in the big double bed.

It had not seemed to Peter that he had taken very long to enter the house and make his way upstairs, but already Mr Fawcett was in bed again, lying there in an attitude of exhaustion, his head and shoulders against piled pillows, his arms outside the bedclothes, hands open with palms upwards. His eyes were shut. The striped dressing-gown, of some soft woollen material, had been discarded and lay rumpled over the bottom part of the bed, like an extra rug.

Peter stood at the foot of the bed, looking at Mr Fawcett. Slowly Mr Fawcett's eyelids went up, and he was looking at Peter. Neither spoke; but each regarded the other with the closest attention.

Peter's hands gripped the bedrail. If the other did not, he must speak. He opened his mouth, but no words suggested themselves. He closed his mouth again.

Barely, Mr Fawcett spoke, his eyes never leaving Peter. He whispered a word, or half a word: 'Rob . . .'

Peter wanted to protest: 'No! I wasn't stealing anything. I came because you beckoned me – you *invited* me. I came straight to you. I've damaged nothing, taken nothing. Nothing.' But still something prevented his speaking.

Mr Fawcett continued to stare at him – glare at him. He muttered a word that sounded like 'robbery'. His eyelids closed then; he turned his head aside on the pillow, as if he had seen enough, spoken enough.

Peter remained where he was, staring. For seconds. For minutes. Would he have been there still, an hour later perhaps – the figure of a boy at the foot of Mr Fawcett's bed, waiting for Mr Fawcett to reopen his old, blurred eyes and see him again?

The house was so quiet that even a slight noise from downstairs resounded: the fumble of a key in the lock of the front door. If he heard, old Mr Fawcett paid no attention; but Peter heard, and fled. But, by the time he had reached the top of the stairs, he could already distinguish footsteps on the tiling of the hall floor: he realized that, if he went down now, he would unavoidably come face to face with – whom?

He turned back, opened the first door he came to, and slipped inside: he was in a bedroom evidently long disused. He closed the door to a crack, and then peeped through the crack. Somebody was now toiling up the stairs: Mrs Pugh, in an overall, and carrying her cleaning tools. Studying her through the crack, Peter saw what his mother meant by 'one foot in the grave': Mrs Pugh looked almost as old and tired as old Mr Fawcett himself.

Once Mrs Pugh had passed and gone into Mr Fawcett's bedroom, Peter could escape. As he tiptoed down the stairs, he heard Mrs Pugh dolefully asking Mr Fawcett whether he'd used the commode in the night, and telling him the weather was bad and so was her sciatica. He heard no more. Back downstairs and through the french windows he went, and across the garden, skulking behind shrubs as much as possible, in case either Mr Fawcett or Mrs Pugh might be looking through the bedroom window. So to the wall, and over it.

He was late for school that day.

For the rest of that day – and for many days after – Peter turned over in his mind what had happened at Fawcett's. He couldn't understand it; he couldn't even understand what there was to understand. Beckoned in; and then – 'robbery' . . . It didn't make sense . . .

He wondered if Mr Fawcett would tell Mrs Pugh about his visitor, Peter. He wondered if he *could* tell Mrs Pugh, since his voice seemed so weak, and she was stone-deaf. He asked his mother.

'I believe the old man writes notes,' she said. 'Although that must be hard for him, because he's half blind by now, they say.' She snorted. 'The stone deaf looking after the half blind! And that daughter willing and able to look after her father, and not allowed into the house!'

Peter could hardly imagine Mr Fawcett's writing a note to Mrs Pugh about a visit as strange as his own, and he could certainly not imagine Mrs Pugh's understanding it. He put anxiety about himself out of his mind.

Then, when Peter had begun to shelve the whole subject, the surprise came. He was fooling about as usual with his friends in the playground of the housing-estate, against Fawcett's wall. He had not been over that wall since his encounter with old Mr Fawcett: he did not intend ever going again. But he sometimes looked speculatively at the wall; and today he saw a boy climbing it – climbing out of Fawcett's. He was the new boy, Davy Taylor, who had arrived at school in the middle of term. A small, quiet boy, pleasant enough; but – he had climbed out of Fawcett's, and Peter, who had been in the playground nearly an hour, had not seen him climb in.

'Here!' said Peter. 'Where've you been?'

'Home to tea,' said Davy Taylor.

'Where?'

'Fawcett's.'

'You don't live there: old Fawcett lives there.'

'I know he does: he's my granddad.'

Peter stared stupidly. 'Old Fawcett lives alone.'

'Not now. He sent for my mum to come and look after him, so we all live there now.'

'Sent for you – *why*?'

'Dunno.' Impatient of the conversation, Davy Taylor slid away into the game being played. Peter was left unanswered.

He believed Davy Taylor – he had to. Yet it was odd . . .

Peter decided to get to know Davy Taylor better. That was easy, because Davy was new and wanted acquaintances and friends. It turned out that he kept gerbils. So did Peter. They swapped information and anecdotes, and they swapped a gerbil or two. Peter found that he liked Davy anyway, so that he was in no hurry to press the friendship to a useful conclusion. In that, he turned out to be wrong: time was short, after all. Peter asked Davy to his house to see his gerbils, and Davy came.

Then Davy asked Peter to Fawcett's to see *his* gerbils, and Peter was going, all agog, when old Mr Fawcett died.

His dying was really no surprise to anybody, Peter discovered: Mr Fawcett was nearly ninety, and the District Nurse had expected him to pop off any day, she said. He made a good end: he had his daughter with him, and he was glad of it.

Some time after the funeral, Davy renewed his invitation to Peter to come and see his gerbils. There was no longer the same point in the visit, of course; but Peter went.

They went from school together. When they reached Fawcett's Davy led the way at breakneck speed through the front door, across the hall, up the stairs to his own room –

'No!' cried Peter, alarmed: Davy's hand was on the knob of the door of old Mr Fawcett's bedroom. But, of course, Davy paid no attention: he flung the door wide, and there was a room newly painted in buttercup yellow, with Davy's narrow bed pushed in one corner, and the rest of the floor space covered with trains and aeroplanes and gerbil cages and gerbils. And that was all.

Except that over the bed was spread something dark striped, silkily warm-looking, that Peter recognized.

'That,' he said.

'What?'

'That stripey thing. That dressing-gown.'

'It's not a dressing-gown. It's a bedspread, sort of.'

'It's a dressing-gown. It must be.'

'It's not.' Davy was cross. He picked the thing up; and Peter could see that it really was not a dressing-gown. On the other hand, it was a very odd bedspread: not large enough, not rectangular, and made up of odd-shaped pieces, with the stripes going all ways. Davy said, 'My granddad used it on his bed. Over the bottom, to keep his feet warm.'

'He used it as a dressing-gown, too,' said Peter. 'He must have, somehow. When he went downstairs, he wrapped it round him. Just a few weeks ago.'

'Don't be silly. He never went downstairs. Not for years. And what do you know about my granddad, anyway? Honestly . . .' Davy was exasperated. 'Honestly . . .'

Peter dropped the subject. They looked at the gerbils, and took them out of their cages and played with them; and after a while Mrs Taylor called them down to tea. The other Taylor children were there – Davy's elder brother and sister. Mrs Taylor had toasted crumpets for everyone, and made sausages and mash and a big pot of tea. Mrs Taylor had hardworking hands and a plain face with a nice smile. When the elder children had gone off to do their homework, she kept Peter at the table, asking about his gerbils and also about his family, whom she remembered a little from long ago. Then Peter and Davy helped her clear the tea-things to the sink, after which Davy said: 'Let's go to the playground, Pete. Everyone'll be there by now.'

Peter cleared his throat. 'You go,' he said. 'I'll come in a bit. I'll help your mother with the washing-up first.'

Davy goggled at him; and even Mrs Taylor was too astonished to be able to look grateful.

'Honestly . . .' said Davy. 'Honestly . . .'

'You go with Davy, Peter,' said Mrs Taylor. 'I can manage. I always do. It's a pity to miss the last of the daylight.'

'No,' said Peter. 'I'll help. But Davy can go.'

Davy hesitated uneasily, then went. Mrs Taylor began washing up; Peter began drying.

For the second time since tea, Peter cleared his throat. 'That stripey thing on Davy's bed: it's nice, but it's a funny thing, isn't it?'

'Well,' said Mrs Taylor. 'It was my mother's dressing-gown – her winter dressing-gown, of a beautiful warm stuff. When she died, it was too good just to let go; but my father wouldn't wear it – a woman's dressing-gown, you know – although it would have fitted him. My mother was a big woman. Anyway, Mrs Pugh was younger in those days, and she unpicked it all and made a half-bedspread of it. It's odd-looking, but warm.'

Peter said: 'It was your mother's dressing-gown . . .'

'She was a remarkable woman,' said Mrs Taylor. 'She could manage most things, and she was patient. She needed to be. My father was difficult. You'll have heard tales . . .'

'Yes,' said Peter. Then, as Mrs Taylor did not go on, he added: 'Mum said you once had a brother, much younger, and he died; and then your father . . .'

'Yes. When he was killed – he was only a boy – my father turned me out of the house, I'm afraid. He swore that he'd not see me in this house again before he saw him, his dead son, I mean. My father prided himself on being a man of his word.'

'He meant never to have you here?'

'Yes. My mother fought him; but it was no good. She said she'd never rest, in this life or the next, till her daughter could come home. It made no difference.'

Peter did not contradict. Changing the subject a little, he asked: 'What was your brother called, that died?'

'Robert.'

'Just Robert?'

'We called him Rob for short. Or Robbie.'

'Yes,' said Peter. 'I see. Now I see.'

Gently Mrs Taylor took the drying-cloth from his hand. 'You've been drying the same plate over and over again, Peter. You go now. I'll finish.'

'Yes,' said Peter. 'Thank you – thank you very much.'

'I'm glad Davy has such a good friend,' said Mrs Taylor. 'Take our short-cut to the playground, Peter. Through the dining-room – I use it for my dressmaking – and through the french windows and across the garden to the wall. That's the way Davy always goes.'

Peter went that way. When he reached the far side of the lawn – hacked short by a mower, since the Taylors had moved in – he stopped to look back at the house. He half-expected to see a tall figure through the french windows, with hand raised for the last time in salutation; in acknowledgement; in thanks.

But nobody.

He went over the wall, into the scrum of boys in the playground, with Davy Taylor in the middle of them.

The Dear Little Man
with His Hands in His Pockets

WHEN I was little, our next-door neighbour was Mr Porter. To begin with, we didn't know him very well; perhaps we never knew him very well. I still wonder about him sometimes.

Mr Porter was a widower, with one married daughter who lived the other side of London. She wanted her father to live with them, but he wouldn't. He preferred to live alone. He wouldn't have even a dog or cat for company.

Mr Porter didn't go out much because he had a bad leg. He said that a lion had chewed it long ago in Africa. He'd certainly spent nearly all his life in Africa – his skin was browned and dried with years and years of sun – but you never knew how much to believe of his stories. He had an eyelid that twitched fairly regularly, and you couldn't be sure whether he was winking, or just twitching, when he said certain things.

Sometimes his chewed leg was painful, and then he had to put it up to rest it. When my mother realized that, she offered to do his shopping for him. Mr Porter accepted her offer very gratefully, and so we got to know Mr Porter better. My mother and father liked Mr Porter. He was always grateful to them, and when we were away on holiday he fed Tibby, our cat, and kept an eye on the house. His married daughter, when she visited him, always called on us and said what a comfort it was to know we were just next

door, and she used to give me the most enormous tubes of Smarties.

I was so little then that wherever my mother went, I went. I used to go with her when she called in to see how Mr Porter was – he'd given her a house-key so that he didn't need even to hobble to the door to let her in. The inside of Mr Porter's house was rather dull, except for one or two African curios.

'Look, Betsy!' said my mother one day, when I'd been fidgeting at the time she was talking with old Mr Porter to make out his shopping list. 'Look, Betsy! A big dolly – look, just behind the door!'

I looked into the shadows behind Mr Porter's sitting-room door, and someone was standing there, about two feet tall, silent and still.

'Not a dolly,' I said.

My mother peered. 'A dear little man with his hands in his pockets,' she said.

'Bring him over here, Betsy,' said Mr Porter, who was sitting with his leg up on a stool.

I wouldn't touch the mannikin, but my mother picked him up for me. Since he had his hands in his pockets, as she put it, his arms formed jug-handles, one on each side of his body. Using one of these handles, my mother carried him over to Mr Porter. He was easy to carry, but evidently quite heavy.

My mother left me with Mr Porter while she went into the kitchen to see what vegetables he had and whether they were fresh enough.

Mr Porter showed me the little man. I think he was made of wood, but the whole of his body, except for his head, was covered in a kind of closely knitted string, rather dirty. He had a face, of sorts; but the most remarkable thing about him was a crown – or perhaps it was meant to be a bush of hair – made of chicken feathers, also rather dingy, and broken at the tips.

'Don't you like him?' asked Mr Porter.

'No,' I said.

'But he makes a true friend. A loyal and determined friend, Betsy. So they used to say in that part of Africa where I got him.' And he said the name of a place so strange-sounding that I paid no attention to it at all; I rather wish now that I could remember it.

'You must realize, Betsy,' said Mr Porter, 'that my friend's not quite as he should be. The shabbiness doesn't matter, but he should have a pair of goat-horns; and, if you wanted him to set off and do your work for you, you'd have to pour a special liquid into him through the feathers on top. See if you can find the hole among the feathers.'

My curiosity got the better of my fear. I parted the feathers here and there and peered down among them, but could see nothing. So I felt with one hand, and – sure enough – there was a hole in the top of the head.

My mother had come back by now with the shopping list, to which she was adding some vegetables. She began to talk to Mr Porter, and he answered her, but he kept his eyes on me.

My hand was still very small in those days, and I put it right into the hole that I had found. The hole went surprisingly deep, and then, at the bottom, my fingers touched a sticky wetness. I drew my hand up again quickly and began wiping it on my anorak.

Mr Porter was watching me all the time, and now he said: 'You never asked me, Betsy, what work such a friendly little chap can do when he gets his stuff inside him.'

'What does he do?'

'Well, you can send him walking off to deal with any enemy you may have.' His eyelid twitched; or he winked.

'What does he *do*?'

'He kills that enemy.'

I stared at the fingers I had been scrubbing at. 'Is it poison then – the liquid? Does he shoot it out of himself at the enemy?'

'Oh, no, no, no,' said Mr Porter. 'The liquid is only like the petrol that makes a car go – although it's much more special and difficult to come by than petrol. No, there are more ways of killing an enemy than by poison, you know . . .'

I think he might have been going to tell me exactly how the little man did his work, but my mother said briskly, 'What a *very* interesting African curio, Mr Porter. Come, Betsy, or we'll never get all the shopping done.' I could tell from her voice that she didn't think Mr Porter was being good for me.

Perhaps my mother was right, for that night I had a nightmare about Mr Porter's little man. I saw him in the distance, walking towards me. I tried to escape him, but his walk broke into a run, swift and steady. In Mr Porter's house I had seen that the little man's hands weren't really in pockets; they just disappeared into his body. But I sup-posed that he could pull them out of his body; and, in the nightmare, coming towards me, he was going to pull them out. What would they be like? Would they be grasping some weapon or weapons? Would they be ordinary hands at all? Or would they be – say – paws, like a lion's paws, only smaller, with deadly claws sheathed in them? Just as he was close to me, and pulling them out, I woke.

I didn't tell my mother about the nightmare, of course; and you might have thought I would have avoided Mr Porter and his friend after that. But there was one way in which Mr Porter – and only Mr Porter – could reassure me about the little man; and so I went with my mother on several further occasions to Mr Porter's house. At last it happened that, for a few minutes, my mother left us alone together.

I said baldly: 'That man couldn't really kill anybody. He's too small. He couldn't even reach.'

Mr Porter understood me at once. 'Reach? Consider your own cat, Betsy. I've seen Tibby at the foot of the garden wall, which is many times her own height – say, five or six feet high. I've seen her look up, crouch, and then spring vertically – vertically, Betsy – to the top. With ease. Right?' I nodded miserably, seeing what he was getting at. 'Now imagine some enemy of mine as tall as six feet. His throat – a very vulnerable part – would be less than that from the ground. My friend has only to walk – or perhaps run ÷ up to him –'

This was so like my nightmare that I closed my eyes. I had to hear Mr Porter's voice going on, but at least I needn't listen to the words he was saying. Then there was another sound: I opened my eyes again, and my mother was re-entering the room from wherever else in the house she had been.

'And so,' Mr Porter was saying, 'just like your Tibby, my friend can easily do what he wants to do. His little job of work, I mean.'

His eyelid twitched; or he winked. He also smiled at my mother in his grateful way.

I took care never to enter into conversation with Mr Porter again on the subject of his friend. If I had to go into Mr Porter's house, I never looked behind the sitting-room door. But I was sure the little man was there. And I used to wonder about the hole among the chicken feathers: whether there was still a sticky wetness at the bottom, or whether it had dried up. Or whether Mr Porter renewed it sometimes. My hand was growing bigger, and I doubted whether I could have squeezed it in, as I had done in the first place, to find out.

I don't know how many years passed before the time of the burglaries in our neighbourhood. Certainly Mr Porter seemed much, much older. There were several burglaries, and the burglary of Mr Porter's house was the last.

Mr Porter still lived alone. Although he wasn't exactly bedridden, he'd had his own bed moved downstairs into his sitting-room, and he spent most of his time lying in it, or on it. His married daughter made more fuss every time she came to see him. But Mr Porter pointed out that he had the telephone by his bed, and he'd promised to ring us at once if he were taken ill or needed help in any way.

One night I was woken by the sound of voices, near and far. The near voice was my mother's in the bedroom next to mine, shouting at my father, who slept soundly: 'Get up – get up! Can't you hear?'

I could hear. From further away, out in the street, came the sound of another voice – or other voices: there was a most terrible screaming and shouting – but not words, at least that one could distinguish – and a deep grunting. Once I did think the screaming was for help.

By now I was in my parents' room. They didn't notice my coming in, because they had thrown the window up and were looking out of it. You couldn't see anything – it was one of those times when the street-lights were on all day and off all night; and there was no moon. (I believe that is the kind of night that burglars usually choose.)

My father said: 'It's a fight.'

'It's a murder!' said my mother. And she dashed at the telephone and began ringing the police.

What was going on out there sounded like a fight *and* a murder. And then, abruptly – just when my father had found his big torch, which was also heavy enough to be a weapon – whatever had been going on was over. There was the sound of running feet – one pair of running feet – and a kind of choking, howling crying that died away with the sound of the feet.

Through all this, by the way, I managed to avoid being noticed by my mother, who would have tried to send me back to bed. I stuck close to my father, and was just behind him when he reached the front-gateway to our house and flashed his torch up and down the street. The whole street had been aroused by the screaming. Windows had been flung up. Many front doors were now open, and silhouetted figures peered out or, like my father, shone torches.

The torch-lights, criss-crossing over the street, showed nobody – and no body, either.

My mother came rushing out from the house behind us and brushed past my father, crying: 'Mr Porter! What about old Mr Porter?' She had a sixth sense about things, sometimes.

My father turned his torch-beam on to Mr Porter's

house. The front door had swung open, and we could see a gaping, jagged hole in the glass of the upper panelling, just above the lock. There was no sign of Mr Porter.

My mother gave a little cry and came back to my father – she must have looked straight at me, but never saw me – and he put his arm round her shoulder, and together they went quickly into Mr Porter's house. I began to follow at a distance, when, out of the corner of my eye, I thought I saw something lying in the darkness of the gutter. I hurried then to catch up closely with my parents. I was very scared indeed.

There was no light in the hall of Mr Porter's house, but there was a light beyond, in the sitting-room where – as you may remember – Mr Porter now slept. The sitting-room door was open, but only just. (It had a spring on it, so that it was self-closing against draughts.) My father gave a push to the door, and we all walked into the sitting-room.

And there was Mr Porter sitting on the side of his bed in his pyjamas, with the telephone receiver in his hand. He was glittering with excitement. Also in his expression was an eagerness which I didn't at first understand.

As soon as he saw us, he called out, 'Come in, come in! I've just been ringing the police, and then I was trying to ring my kind next-door neighbours, as I've always promised.'

My mother said, 'Oh, Mr Porter! We thought you'd been murdered in your bed.' Tears began to run down her cheeks.

'There, there!' said Mr Porter. 'Only a burglar – not even a very brave one. Didn't expect to find me in the first room he tried. Didn't expect to find me ready for him.' His eyelid twitched; or he winked. 'Shock of his life. Ran for it.'

Behind us other neighbours had begun trickling into the house. Mr Porter appealed eagerly to this little crowd: 'Well, did he get right away, or did someone – I mean, one of you, of course – catch him? No? No sign of him?'

But everyone agreed that the burglar had got clean away; and, according to Mr Porter, he had taken nothing with him from the house.

'Except this.' Another neighbour pushed through the rest of us to reach Mr Porter. 'Isn't this one of your African ornaments, Mr Porter? It was lying in the gutter, just along the street.' He held out the little man with the jug-handle arms.

'Well, fancy a burglar taking my little man!' said Mr Porter, staring. The little man was filthy with mud from the gutter, and with a lot of blood on him. My mother, returning from the kitchen with a cup of tea for Mr Porter, exclaimed in disgust at the sight.

My father said: 'The blood must be from the burglar's cutting himself on broken glass. He broke the glass in the front door so that he could reach in and open the door from the inside. The police will certainly want to see this thing.'

He took the little man and – not realizing that he was able to stand on his own two feet – leaned him temporarily against the wall. I wondered if Mr Porter would tell the police, when they came, that the little man usually stood behind the sitting-room door, and whether they would think it odd that a burglar, coming in, should reach right round the door to take him.

But when the police came, very soon afterwards, we heard nothing, because we were all turned out of the house while they talked to Mr Porter. We left Mr Porter in bed, sipping his tea, and looking as peaceful and contented as our cat, Tibby, when she suns herself on the top of the garden wall. A policeman sat by the bed with his notebook open, asking questions. I suppose you might say that Mr Porter was helping the police with their inquiries.

My father said the police's best clue would be the blood. He said they would ask all the hospitals to look out for a man coming in with severe glass-cuts on hands, wrists, or arms. They may have done so; but the burglar was never caught. Moreover, nobody was ever able to explain what all the screaming had been about in the street. Nor why there was blood in the gutter and in the street, but not by the front door where the glass had been broken.

When Mr Porter's married daughter heard of the burglary, she said this settled it and her father was coming to live with them. Mr Porter was surprisingly meek, and agreed. So there had to be a big clear-out of Mr Porter's house, because he couldn't take all his things with him to his daughter's home. And then one day Mr Porter went off in his daughter's car, and we never saw him again, although my mother had a nice letter from him, saying how kind we'd been and how much he missed us. For several years we had Christmas cards and then they stopped coming. I suppose he died. He was very old.

I don't know what happened to the little man with his hands in his pockets when the police had finished with him. He was so filthy with mud and blood that perhaps Mr Porter's daughter burnt him: the chicken feathers would have made a terrible smell. Or perhaps she cleaned him up and let Mr Porter stand him behind the door of his new bedroom.

When my father said about the hospitals looking out for a man with wrist-cuts from broken glass, I thought they would have done better to look out for a man suffering from severe throat-wounds. I know we were Mr Porter's friends, not his enemies, but, all the same, I was quite glad when we weren't next-door neighbours any more.

The Dog Got Them

WHEN Captain Joel Jones retired from the sea, he was persuaded by his wife to buy a handy little bungalow in the middle of nowhere in particular. Here the two of them lived very quietly – but with a certain amount of mystery. At least, to Andy Potter, their grandnephew, there was mystery.

Andy knew Aunt Enid fairly well – really, she was Great-Aunt Enid, of course: she used to visit her relations while the Captain was at sea. She was kind, but very prim. She liked to help with the washing-up, mending of clothes, ironing – anything; but she and the Captain had had no children, and she exclaimed a good deal at the noisiness of Andy's friends and the language that young people used nowadays.

Captain Joel was another matter altogether. Andy had met him only rarely, on his return from voyages: a big, red-faced, restless man with a loud voice. (Andy's mother complained privately about *his* language.) When he drank tea, he picked up and set down the cup with a good deal of rattling of china against china. In excuse, he said that he was rather unfamiliar with tea as a beverage. He liked to carry Andy's father off for an evening at the pub. He was always sociable, and said that the Potters must all come and stay in the new bungalow, when they had moved in. There would be two bedrooms: he and Aunt Enid would use one, of course, but Andy's parents could have the other, and

Andy himself, being still a little boy, could sleep on the sofa in the sitting-room. Andy could even bring his terrier puppy, Teaser, if he were careful about the Jones's cat.

They moved in; but, oddly, the invitation to the Potters was never renewed.

Mrs Potter said, 'It's not as if I particularly *want* to stay; but all the same I wonder they don't press us to go. Aunt Enid's so often stayed here; and the Captain, too – and I could have done without the smell of whiskey in the bed-room cupboard afterwards.'

Mr Potter said, 'It'll take some time for them to settle down. Especially for Joel: no sea, no shipmates, no pub near, no company of any kind except Aunt Enid's.'

'You make it sound a bad move for them.'

'Well . . .'

Andy listened, without paying much attention.

Over a year later, on their way back from a holiday by car, the Potters found that they would be passing quite close to the new bungalow. They decided to drop in – and not to telephone ahead about the visit in case, as Mrs Potter said, the answer was, Not at home.

They parked the car outside the bungalow and all got out – all except Teaser. He was left in the car, chiefly because of the Jones's old tabby. In a harmless way, Teaser was always on the look-out for cats. He loved any chase – no doubt, would have loved any fight, too. He came of a breed once specialist in ratting.

They rang the doorbell. From inside they could hear some exclamation of dismay (was it Aunt Enid's voice?) and a much louder, violent exclamation, undoubtedly in the Captain's voice. There was the sound of light footsteps, and the front door was opened.

'Oh, dear!' cried Aunt Enid, on seeing them. 'Oh, dear, oh, dear! How very nice to see you all!'

She did not move from the doorway.

Mrs Potter said: 'We were just passing, Aunt Enid. We thought we'd call to see how you'd settled in. Just a very brief visit.' As Aunt Enid said nothing, Mrs Potter added for her: 'Just time for a quick cup of tea, perhaps, and a chat.'

'Of course!' said Aunt Enid. 'How very nice! But it's not at all suitable, I'm afraid. The Captain is in bed with influenza. Severe influenza.'

There was a roar from inside the bungalow: 'Enid! I say, Enid!'

'There's my patient calling!' cried Aunt Enid. 'Perhaps another time, when he's stronger . . . But telephone first.' To everyone's astonishment, she began to close the door.

Mr Potter put his foot in the doorway. 'Aunt Enid,' he said, 'we don't want to come where we're not wanted for any reason; but – you're all right, aren't you?'

'Oh, perfectly, perfectly!' cried Aunt Enid. 'I'm perfectly all right, and so is the Captain. He is in perfect health. It's just that, with infection in the house, I simply cannot – *cannot* risk having visitors. I admit only the doctor, ever.' She stooped and put her hands round Mr Potter's leg to lift it from the doorway. He withdrew it to save her trouble.

Aunt Enid was in the act of shutting the front door. Mrs Potter said quickly: 'Aunt Enid, promise to let us know at once if we can help you at any time, in any way.'

Aunt Enid's face still showed in the gap of the doorway. Her eyes filled with tears. 'My dear, you are truly kind,' she said. Then, 'But no help is required. I have the Captain, you know.' This time she finished shutting the front door. They heard her 'Good-bye' from the other side.

They went back to the car in silence. As they were driving off, Andy's mother said, 'She looked so worried and miserable. It couldn't be just the Captain's flu.'

'She didn't even seem certain that he *was* ill,' said Andy's father.

And Andy said, 'He wasn't in bed. I looked past Aunt Enid, when you were talking. I saw him. He wasn't even in pyjamas.'

'What was he doing?'

'Just walking about, in a wandery sort of way. Waving something about in the air.'

'Waving what?'

'I think it was a bottle.'

Later, when they got home, Mrs Potter wrote to Aunt Enid, and then she began writing regularly, once a fortnight. Occasionally she had a reply. She would pass it to Andy's father to read, but never read it aloud to them all. Andy wondered.

Then, after many months, Aunt Enid wrote to say that Captain Joel had died.

'What did he die of?' asked Andy.

His parents looked at him thoughtfully, sizing him up, Andy knew: was he old enough to be told whatever it was?

'Yes,' said his mother, 'you're old enough to know; and it should be a warning to you all your life: Captain Joel drank.'

'So does Dad,' said Andy. 'You mean, more than that?'

'He drank much more,' said his father. 'He drank much, much too much. He died of it.'

'Oh,' said Andy. There was a mystery gone, it seemed.

After the funeral, which Mr and Mrs Potter attended, Aunt Enid came to stay for a bit. She was pale, thin, and apt to burst into tears for no clear reason. Andy's mother gave her breakfast in bed during her stay, and would not let her help as much as usual with the housework. She had long private talks with her, after which they both seemed to have been crying.

'Poor woman,' said Andy's mother, when Aunt Enid had gone. 'It was a perfectly dreadful time when the Captain was dying. Appalling.'

'DTs?' asked Andy's father.

His mother nodded.

Andy asked what DTs were.

'*Delirium tremens*,' said his mother. 'A particularly awful kind of deliriousness, from drinking too much for too long. You see things. It's a waking nightmare, according to Aunt Enid.' She shuddered. 'Horrible.'

In due course a letter arrived from Aunt Enid thanking them all for her stay, and saying that she felt much better as a result. She had the energy now to start getting the house to rights again after the Captain's death. She had already changed his sick-room back into a spare-room. 'But,' she said, 'I'm not sure that they've faded yet.'

'They?' Andy's mother queried, passing the letter to her husband.

'Mistake for *it*, I suppose,' said Mr Potter, studying the letter. '*It* being the smell of booze, or something like that.'

'Her letter says *they* quite clearly,' said Andy, also looking.

'Makes no sense,' said his father; and the subject was dropped.

In the next letter Aunt Enid was very much upset because the cat had died. The cat had grown very old and poor in health; but, mysteriously, Aunt Enid seemed to blame herself for its death. She said that it had had a shock which she ought to have been able to spare it, and she thought this shock had caused its death. She had not closely enough supervised where the cat had gone in the house – 'But you don't supervise where a cat goes about indoors, to spare it shock,' said Andy's father.

The next letter was written from hospital. Aunt Enid had fallen and broken her hip, running too fast on the polished floors in the bungalow. She explained briefly: 'I was afraid of not getting the door shut in time.'

'Why should she be running to *shut doors in time*?' Andy's father asked crossly. He foresaw upheavals, if Aunt Enid were in hospital.

He was right. Mrs Potter telephoned to the hospital to suggest a visit; and they had an express letter from Aunt Enid to say that she was looking forward to seeing them at the weekend and suggesting that they stayed overnight in the bungalow. Andy's father and mother could sleep in the double bed in Aunt Enid's room; Andy himself could sleep on the sofa in the sitting-room. If they had to bring Teaser, she did not advise that he came indoors at all: could he not sleep in the car and be exercised from there? She was sorry that the spare-room was not yet habitable: she did not think they had faded yet. The key to the bungalow would be in the milk-box by the back door.

'This fading:' said Andy's father. '*What is she talking about?*' He was exasperated. However, he agreed that they should all go down, as Aunt Enid had suggested, and they did.

The bungalow was neat and clean, as one would have expected of Aunt Enid's home; but it seemed empty and lifeless with even the cat dead. They decided to leave Teaser mostly in the car, as Aunt Enid had wished it. Andy's parents would sleep in Aunt Enid's own room; but what about Andy? It was all very well for Aunt Enid to suggest the sofa: she had forgotten how time had passed – how much older Andy was, how much bigger. So they discussed the suitability of Aunt Enid's spare-room, after all.

Standing in the spare-room, looking around, they could see nothing against its use. Like the rest of the bungalow, it was neat and clean, with a single bed and a bedside lamp that worked. The room had no special features. There was a chiming clock on the mantelpiece – at least, Andy's mother said that it used to chime, but it had stopped working altogether by now. (Andy tried to wind it, in vain.) There was a cactus in a pot on the window sill, and a white china rabbit heading a procession of little white china rabbits on a dressing-table.

'Why didn't she want us to use the room?' Andy's mother asked suspiciously. They had a good look round. Nothing odd; and absolutely no trace left of the late Captain Joel, except for an empty whiskey bottle that Andy spotted, poked up the chimney.

Andy decided for himself by unrolling his sleeping-bag on the single bed.

After supper, they all went to bed.

Andy woke up in what seemed the middle of the night, but the room was not really dark. He thought he had been woken by a noise: a squeaking, perhaps. Now he was almost sure there was a soft scrabbling sound from the floor beyond the bottom of the bed. Very quietly he raised himself on his elbow to look. Against the far wall, heads together as if conferring, were two rats. They must be rats, and yet they were much, much larger than any ordinary rat, and their colour was a grey white splotched with chestnut brown. He disliked their colouring very much. They seemed to have heard the slight creak of Andy's bed-springs, for now they turned their heads to look at him. They had pink eyes.

Then they began creeping to and fro against the wall, and then running, in an agitated kind of way, almost as if they were getting their courage up. Each time they ran in the direction of the bed, they ran nearer than they had done the last time. Especially the bigger of the two rats, which Andy assumed to be the male. The female lagged behind a little, always; but still she ran a little nearer to the bed every time.

The male rat was scurrying closer and closer, and suddenly the knowledge came to Andy that it was going to attack. He was appalled. Frantically he prepared to ward off its attack with his naked hand. The rat sprang, launching its heavy body through the air like a missile, and sank its teeth into his hand.

Andy was already on his feet on the bed. He knew the female rat would attack next. The male hung from his hand as he slapped it violently, madly, repeatedly against the wall so that the body of the iron-teethed monster banged again and again and again against the wall. It seemed to him that almost simultaneously the body of the rat suddenly flew from its head, still teeth-clenched in his flesh, and he himself flew from that dreadful bedroom. He slammed the door behind him against the female rat, and rushed into his

parents' room. They had already put on the light, roused by his screaming.

Andy was still screaming: 'Look! The rat – the rat!' He held out his hand for them to see the horror hanging from it.

They all looked at his hand: Andy's brown right hand, just as it always had been, entirely unmarked except where he had once scarred himself with a saw long ago. No rat.

'You've been dreaming,' said his mother. 'You were asleep and you had a nightmare.'

'No,' said Andy, 'I was awake.' And he told them everything.

They went back into the spare-room with him. There were no rats of course, nor any sign of one.

Staring round, Andy's father said at last, 'They weren't your rats, Andy; they were the Captain's. And, as your Great-Aunt said, they haven't faded yet.'

They shut the door fast on the spare-room, and made up a bed of sorts for Andy in the sitting-room, with cushions on the floor and then his sleeping-bag on top. Then they all went back to bed.

But – not surprisingly, perhaps – Andy could not get to sleep. He found that he was listening for sounds behind the door of the spare-room. In the end he got up quietly and went out of the bungalow and brought Teaser in from the car for company. Teaser was delighted.

Andy had begun to fall asleep with the comforting weight of Teaser on his feet, when the dog left him. He was slipping out of the sitting-room, whose door had been deliberately left ajar: Andy called softly, but Teaser paid no attention. Andy got up and followed him. By now Teaser was across the hall and at the spare-room door. His nose was at the bottom crack, moving to and fro along it, sampling the air there. His tail moved occasionally, stiffly, in pleasure or in pleasurable anticipation.

Andy thought he heard a squeak from the other side of the door: *two* squeaks: the squeaks of two different rat voices.

'No, Teaser,' whispered Andy. 'Oh, no!'

But Teaser looked over his shoulder at Andy, and his look spoke. On impulse Andy opened the spare-room door a few inches, and at once Teaser had pushed past it into the room.

Instantly there was tumult – a wild barking and the rush of scuttering feet and objects falling and crashing and breaking and the clock that never went now chiming on and on in horological frenzy. Above all, the joyous barking of chase and battle.

Andy held the door to, without clicking it shut, in case Teaser might want to get out in a hurry. But Teaser did not want to get out: he was in a terrier's paradise.

By now Andy's father and mother were out of bed again, with Andy, and he explained what he had done. Mr Potter was of the opinion that they should wait outside the room until Teaser had finished doing whatever he was doing. Mrs Potter insisted that, in the meantime, Mr Potter should fetch the poker from the sitting-room. Then they waited until the barking and worrying noises grew less frequent. A kind of peace seemed to have come to the spare-room.

Mr Potter flung wide the door, at the same time switching the light on.

The room was in a terrible mess: the bedspread had been torn off the bed, and the floor-rugs were in a heap in one corner; the china rabbit and its litter were smashed and scattered all over the room; the cactus stood on its head in the middle of the floor, with earth and potsherds widely strewn round it; and the clock had been hurled from the mantelpiece and lay face downwards on the floor in a mess of broken glass, still chiming. On the bed stood Teaser, panting, his mouth wide open with his tongue hanging out, his tail briskly wagging, his eyes shining. He was radiant, triumphant. The night of his life.

After a silence, '*They* won't come back,' said Mr Potter, 'ever.'

They tidied the bedroom as best they could. They repotted the cactus and threw away the remains of the rabbits, and put the clock back on the mantelpiece. It would need a new glass, of course, but it had stopped chiming and was ticking quite sensibly. Mrs Potter set it to the right time – nearly breakfast time.

Later that day, visiting Aunt Enid in hospital, Andy apologized for Teaser about the rabbits and the clock-glass. He did not explain things. His mother had said that it would be best not to burden the invalid with the whole story.

Aunt Enid was not as prim as she used to be. She was naturally confused about what had been going on in the bungalow; but pleased. 'I'm pleased that you and the dog had such a nice romp, Andy dear,' she said. 'And when I'm home again, it'll be a great convenience that the clock really goes. I can easily get a new glass.' She hesitated. 'You had no trouble from – from *them*?'

Andy's father said quickly: 'The dog got them.'

The Strange Illness
of Mr Arthur Cook

ON a cold, shiny day at the end of winter the Cook family
went to look at the house they were likely to buy. Mr and
Mrs Cook had viewed it several times before, and had
discussed it thoroughly; this was a first visit for their children, Judy and Mike.

Also with the Cooks was Mr Biley, of the house-agent's
firm of Ketch, Robb and Biley in Walchester.

'Why's *he* come?' whispered Judy. (And, although the
Cooks were not to know this, Mr Biley did not usually
accompany clients in order to clinch deals.)

Her parents shushed Judy.

They had driven a little way out of Walchester into the
country. The car now turned down a lane which, perhaps
fifty years before, had been hardly more than a farm-track.
Now there were several houses along it. The lane came to a
dead end at a house with a *For Sale* notice at its front gate.
On the gate itself was the name of the house: Southcroft.

'There it is!' said Mr Arthur Cook to his two children.

'And very nice, too!' Mr Biley said enthusiastically.

But, in fact, the house was not particularly nice. In size it
was small to medium; brick-built, slate-roofed; exactly rectangular; and rather bleak-looking. It stood in the middle
of a large garden, also exactly rectangular and rather bleak-
looking.

Mike, who tended to like most things that happened to

him, said: 'Seems O.K.' He was gazing round not only at the house and its garden, but at the quiet lane – ideal for his bike – and at the surrounding countryside. It would be all far, far better than where they were living now, in Walchester.

Judy, who was older than Mike, and the only one in the family with a sharply pointed, inquisitive nose, said nothing – yet. She looked round alertly, intently.

'Nice big garden for kids to play in,' Mr Biley pointed out.

'I might even grow a few vegetables,' said Mr Cook.

'Oh, Arthur!' his wife said, laughing.

'Well,' Mr Cook said defensively, 'I haven't had much chance up to now, have I?' In Walchester the Cooks had only a paved backyard. But, anyway, Mr Cook, whose job was fixing television aerials on to people's roofs, had always said that in his spare-time he wanted to be indoors in an easy chair.

'Anyway,' said Mr Biley, as they went in by the front gate, 'you've lovely soil here. Still in good tilth.'

'Tilth?' said Mr Cook.

'That's it,' said Mr Biley.

They reached the front door. Mr Biley unlocked it, and they all trooped in.

Southcroft had probably been built some time between the two wars. There was nothing antique about it, nor anything of special interest at all. On the other hand, it all appeared to be in good order, even to the house's having been fairly recently redecorated.

The Cooks went everywhere, looked everywhere, their footsteps echoing uncomfortably in empty rooms. They reassembled in the sitting-room, which had french windows letting on to the garden at the back. Tactfully Mr Biley withdrew into the garden to leave the family to private talk.

'Well, there you are,' said Mr Cook. 'Just our size of house. Not remarkable in any way, but snug, I fancy.'

'Remarkable in one way, Arthur,' said his wife. 'Remarkably cheap.'

'A snip,' agreed Mr Cook.

'Why's it so cheap?' asked Judy.

'You ask too many questions beginning with *why*,' said her father, but good-humouredly.

It was true, however, that there seemed no particular reason for the house being as cheap as it was. Odd, perhaps.

'Can't we go into the garden now?' asked Mike.

Mike and Judy went out, and Mr Biley came in again.

There wasn't much for the children to see in the garden. Close to the house grew unkempt grass, with a big old apple tree – the only tree in the garden – which Mike began to climb very thoroughly. The rest of the garden had all been under cultivation at one time, but now it was neglected, a mess of last season's dead weeds. There were some straggly bushes – raspberry canes, perhaps. There had once been a greenhouse: only the brick foundations were left. There was a garden shed, and behind it a mass of stuff which Judy left Mike to investigate. She wanted to get back to the adult conversation.

By the time Judy rejoined the party indoors there was no doubt about it: the Cooks were buying the house. Mr Biley was extremely pleased, Judy noticed. He caught Judy staring at him and jollily, but very unwisely, said: 'Well, young lady?'

Judy, invited thus to join in the conversation, had a great

many questions to ask. She knew she wouldn't be allowed to ask them all, and she began almost at random: 'Who used to live here?'

'A family called Cribble,' said Mr Biley. 'A very *nice* family called Cribble.'

'Cribble,' Judy repeated to herself, storing the piece of information away. 'And why –'

At that moment Mike walked in again from the garden. 'There's lots of stuff behind the shed,' he said. 'Rolls and rolls of chicken wire, in an awful mess, and wood – posts and slats and stuff.'

'Easily cleared,' said Mr Biley. 'The previous owners were going to have bred dogs, I believe. They would have erected sheds, enclosures, runs – all that kind of thing.'

'Why did the Cribbles give up the idea?' asked Judy.

Mr Biley looked uneasy. 'Not the Cribbles,' he said, 'the Johnsons. The family here before the Cribbles.'

'Why did the Johnsons give up the idea, then?' asked Judy. 'I mean, when they'd got all the stuff for it?'

'They –' Mr Biley appeared to think deeply, if only momentarily: 'They had to move rather unexpectedly.'

'Why?'

'Family reasons, perhaps?' said Mrs Cook quickly. She knew some people found Judy tiresome.

'Family reasons, no doubt,' Mr Biley agreed.

Judy said thoughtfully to herself: 'The Johnsons didn't stay long enough to start dog-breeding, and they went in such a hurry that they left their stuff behind. The Cribbles came, but they didn't stay long enough to have time to clear away all the Johnsons' stuff. I wonder why *they* left . . .'

Nobody could say that Judy was asking Mr Biley a question, but he answered her all the same. 'My dear young lady,' he said, in a manner so polite as to be also quite rude, 'I do not know why. Nor is it my business.' He sounded as if he did not think it was Judy's either. He turned his back on her and began talking loudly about house-purchase to Mr Cook.

Judy was not put out. She had investigated mysteries and secrets before this and she knew that patience was all-important.

The Cooks bought Southcroft and moved in almost at once. Spring came late that year, and in the continuing cold weather the house proved as snug as one could wish. When the frosts were over, the family did some work outside, getting rid of all the dog-breeding junk: they made a splendid bonfire of the wood, and put the wire out for the dustmen. Mr Cook took a long look at the weeds beginning to sprout everywhere, and groaned. He bought a fork and spade and hoe and rake and put them into the shed.

In their different ways the Cooks were satisfied with the move. The new house was still convenient for Mr Cook's work. Mrs Cook found that the neighbours kept themselves to themselves more than she would have liked, but she got a part-time job in a shop in the village, and *that* was all right. Mike made new friends in the new school, and they went riding round the countryside on their bikes. Judy was slower at making friends, because she was absorbed in her own affairs. Particularly in investigation, in which she was disappointed for a time. She could find out so little about the Cribbles and the Johnsons: why they had stayed so briefly at Southcroft, why they had moved in so much haste. The Cribbles now lived the other side of Walchester, rather smartly, in a house with a large garden which they had had expensively landscaped. (Perhaps the size of the garden at Southcroft was what had attracted them to the house in the first place. In the village people said that the Cribbles had already engaged landscape-garden specialists for Southcroft, when they suddenly decided to leave.) As for the Johnsons, Judy discovered that they had moved right away, to Yorkshire, to do their dog-breeding. Before the Cribbles and the Johnsons, an old couple called Baxter had lived in the house for many years, until one had died and the other moved away.

The Cooks had really settled in. Spring brought sunshine and longer days; and it also brought the first symptoms of Mr Cook's strange illness.

At first the trouble seemed to be his eyesight. He complained of a kind of brownish fog between himself and the television screen. He couldn't see clearly enough to enjoy the programmes. He thought he noticed that this fogginess was worse when he was doing daylight viewing, at the weekends or in the early evening. He tried to deal with this by drawing the curtains in the room where the set was on, but the fogginess persisted.

Mr Cook went to the optician to see whether he needed glasses. The optician applied all the usual tests, and said that Mr Cook's vision seemed excellent. Mr Cook said it wasn't – or, at least, sometimes wasn't. The optician said that eyesight could be affected by a person's state of general health, and suggested that, if the trouble continued, Mr Cook should consult a doctor.

Mr Cook was annoyed at the time he had wasted at the optician's, and went home to try to enjoy his favourite Saturday afternoon programme. Not only did he suffer from increased fogginess of vision, but – perhaps as a result, perhaps not – he developed a splitting headache. In the end he switched the set off and went outside and savagely dug in the garden, uprooting ground elder, nettle, twitch and a great number of other weed species. By teatime he had cleared a large patch, in which Judy at once sowed radishes and mustard and cress.

At the end of an afternoon's digging, the headache had gone. Mr Cook was also able to watch the late night movie on television without discomfort. But his Saturday as a whole had been ruined; and when he went to bed, his sleep was troubled by strange dreams, and on Sunday morning he woke at first light. This had become the pattern of his sleeping recently: haunted dreams and early wakings. On this particular occasion, as often before, he couldn't get to sleep again; and he spent the rest of Sunday – a breezy, sunny day – moving restlessly about indoors from Sunday paper to television set, saying he felt awful.

Mrs Cook said that perhaps he ought to see a doctor, as the optician had advised; Mr Cook shouted at her that he wouldn't.

But, as spring turned to summer, it became clear that something would have to be done. Mr Cook's condition was worsening. He gave up trying to watch television. Regularly he got up at sunrise because he couldn't sleep longer and couldn't even rest in bed. (Sometimes he went out and dug in the garden; and, when he did so, the exertion or the fresh air seemed to make him feel better, at least for the time being.) He lost his appetite; and he was always irritable with his children. He grumbled at Mike for being out so much on his bicycle, and he grumbled at Judy for being at home. Her investigations no longer amused him at all. Judy had pointed out that his illness seemed to vary with the weather: fine days made it worse. She wondered why. Her father said he'd give her *why*, if she weren't careful.

At last Mrs Cook burst out that she could stand this no longer: 'Arthur, you *must* go to the doctor.' As though he had only been waiting for someone to insist, Mr Cook agreed.

The doctor listened carefully to Mr Cook's account of his symptoms and examined him thoroughly. He asked whether he smoked and whether he ate enough roughage. Reassured on both these points, the doctor said he thought Mr Cook's condition might be the result of nervous tension. 'Anything worrying you?' asked the doctor.

'Of course, there is!' exploded Mr Cook. 'I'm ill, aren't I? I'm worried sick about that!'

The doctor asked if there was anything else that Mr Cook worried about: his wife? his children? his job?

'I lie awake in the morning and worry about them all,' said Mr Cook. 'And about that huge garden in that awful state . . .'

'What garden?'

'Our garden. It's huge and it's been let go wild and I ought to get it in order, I suppose, and – oh, I don't know! I'm no gardener.'

'Perhaps you shouldn't have a garden that size,' suggested the doctor. 'Perhaps you should consider moving into a house with no garden, or at least a really manageable one. Somewhere, say, with just a patio, in Walchester.'

'That's what we moved *from*,' said Mr Cook. 'Less than six months ago.'

'Oh, dear!' said the doctor. He called Mrs Cook into the surgery and suggested that her husband might be suffering from overwork. Mr Cook was struck by the idea; Mrs Cook less so. The doctor suggested a week off, to see what *that* would do.

That week marked the climax of Mr Cook's illness; it drove Mrs Cook nearly out of her wits, and Judy to urgent inquiries.

The week came at the very beginning of June, an ideal month in which to try to recover from overwork. Judy and Mike were at school all day, so that everything was quiet at home for their father. The sun shone, and Mr Cook planned to sit outside in a deckchair and catch up on lost sleep. Then, when the children came home, he would go to bed early with the portable television set. (He assumed that rest would be dealing with fogginess of vision.)

Things did not work out like that at all. During that week Mr Cook was seized with a terrible restlessness. It seemed impossible for him to achieve any repose at all. He tried only once to watch television; and Judy noticed that thereafter he seemed almost – yes, he seemed afraid. He was a shadow of his former self when, at the end of the week, he went back to work.

After he had left the house that morning, Mrs Cook spoke her fears: 'It'll be the hospital next, I know. And once they begin injecting and cutting up – Oh, why did we ever come to live here!'

'You think it's something to do with the house?' asked Judy. Mike had already set off to school; she lingered.

'Well, your dad was perfectly all right before. I'd say there was something wrong with the drains here, but there's no smell; and, anyway, why should only he fall ill?'

'There is something wrong with the house,' said Judy. 'I couldn't ask the Johnsons about it, so I asked the Cribbles.'

'The Cribbles! That we bought the house from?'

'Yes. They live the other side of Walchester. I went there –'

'Oh, Judy!' said her mother. 'You'll get yourself into trouble with your questions, one of these days.'

'No, I shan't,' said Judy (and she never did). 'I went to ask them about this house. I rang at the front door, and Mrs Cribble answered it. At least, I think it must have been her. She was quite nice. I told her my name, but I don't think she connected me with buying the house from them. Then I asked her about the house, whether *they* had noticed anything.'

'And what did she say?'

'She didn't say anything. She slammed the door in my face.'

'Oh, Judy!' cried Mrs Cook, and burst into tears.

Her mother's tears decided Judy: she would beard Mr Biley himself, of Ketch, Robb and Biley. She was not so innocent as to suppose he would grant her, a child, an official interview. But if she could buttonhole him somewhere, she might get from him at least one useful piece of information.

After school that day, Judy presented herself at the offices of Ketch, Robb and Biley in Walchester. She had her deception ready. 'Has my father been in to see Mr Biley yet?' she asked. That sounded respectable. The receptionist said that Mr Biley was talking with a client at present, and that she really couldn't say –

'I'll wait,' said Judy, like a good girl.

Judy waited. She was prepared to wait until the offices shut at half past five, when Mr Biley would surely leave to go home; but much earlier than that, Mr Biley came downstairs with someone who was evidently rather an important client. Mr Biley escorted him to the door, chatting in the jovial way that Judy remembered so well. They said good-bye at the door, and parted, and Mr Biley started back by the way he had come.

Judy caught up with him, laid a hand on his arm: 'Mr Biley – please!'

Mr Biley turned. He did not recognize Judy. He smiled. 'Yes, young lady?'

'We bought Southcroft from the Cribbles,' she began.

Mr Biley's smile vanished instantly. He said, 'I should make clear at once that Ketch, Robb and Biley will not, under any circumstances, handle that property again.'

'Why?' asked Judy. She couldn't help asking.

'The sale of the same property three times in eighteen months may bring income to us, but it does not bring reputation. So I wish you good day.'

Judy said, '*Please*, I only need to ask you one thing, really.' She gripped the cloth of his sleeve. The receptionist had looked up to see what was going on, and Mr Biley was aware of that. 'Well? Be quick,' he said.

'Before the Cribbles and the Johnsons, there were the Baxters: when old Mr Baxter died, where did Mrs Baxter move to?'

'Into Senior House, Waddington Road.' He removed Judy's fingers from his coat-sleeve. 'Remember to tell your father *not* to call in Ketch, Robb and Biley for the resale of the property. Good-bye.'

It was getting late, but Judy thought she should finish the job. She found a telephone box and the right money and rang her mother to say she was calling on Mrs Baxter in the Old People's flats in Waddington Road. She was glad that her telephone-time ran out before her mother could say much in reply.

Then she set off for Waddington Road.

By the time she reached the flats, Judy felt tired, thirsty, hungry. There was no problem about seeing Mrs Baxter. The porter told her the number of Mrs Baxter's flatlet, and said Mrs Baxter would probably be starting her tea. The residents had just finished seeing a film on mountaineering in the Alps, and – as he put it – would be brewing up late.

Judy found the door and knocked. A delicious smell of hot-buttered toast seemed to be coming through the key-hole. A thin little voice told her to come in. And there sat Mrs Baxter behind a tea-pot with a cosy on it, in the act of spreading honey on a piece of buttered toast.

'Oh,' said Judy, faintly.

Mrs Baxter was delighted to have a visitor. 'Sit down, dear, and I'll get another cup and saucer and plate.'

She was such a nice little old woman, with gingery-grey hair – she wore a gingery dress almost to match – and rather dark pop-eyes. She seemed active, but a bit slow. When she got up in a slow, plump way to get the extra china, Judy was reminded of a hamster she had once had, called Pickles.

Mrs Baxter got the china and some biscuits and poured out another cup of tea. All this without asking Judy her name or her business.

'Sugar?' asked Mrs Baxter.

'Yes, please,' said Judy. 'I'm Judy Cook, Mrs Baxter.'

'Oh, yes? I'll have to get the tin of sugar. I don't take sugar myself, you know.'

She waddled over to some shelves. She had her back to Judy, but Judy could see the little hamster-hands reaching up to a tin marked *Sugar*.

'Mrs Baxter, we live in the house you used to live in: Southcroft.'

The hamster-hands never reached the sugar tin, but stayed up in the air for as long as it might have taken Judy to count ten. It was as though the name Southcroft had turned the little hamster-woman to stone.

Then the hands came down slowly, and Mrs Baxter waddled back to the tea-table. She did not look at Judy; her face was expressionless.

'Have a biscuit?' she said to Judy.

Judy took one. 'Mrs Baxter, I've come to ask you about Southcroft.'

'Don't forget your cup of tea, dear.'

'No, I won't. Mrs Baxter, I must ask you several things –'

'Just a minute dear.'

'Yes?'

'Perhaps you take sugar in your tea?'

'Yes, I do, but it doesn't matter. I'd rather you'd let me ask you –'

'But it does matter,' said Mrs Baxter firmly. 'And I shall get the sugar for you. I don't take it myself, you know.'

Judy had had dreams when she had tried to do something and could not because things – the same things – happened over and over again to prevent her. Now she watched Mrs Baxter waddle over to the shelves, watched the little hamster-hands reach up to the sugar-tin and – this time – bring it down and bring it back to the tea-table. Judy sugared her tea, and took another biscuit, and began eating and drinking. She was trying to steady herself and fortify herself for what she now realized was going to be very, very difficult. Mrs Baxter had begun telling her about mountaineering in the Alps. The little voice went on and on, until Judy thought it must wear out.

It paused.

Judy said swiftly: 'Tell me about Southcroft, please. What was it like to live in when you were there? Why is it so awful now?'

'No, dear,' said Mrs Baxter hurriedly. 'I'd rather go on telling you about the Matterhorn.'

'I want to know about Southcroft,' cried Judy.

'No,' said Mrs Baxter. 'I never talk about it. Never. I'll go on about the Matterhorn.'

'Please. You must tell me about Southcroft.' Judy was insisting, but she knew she was being beaten by the soft little old woman. She found she was beginning to cry. 'Please, Mrs Baxter. My dad's ill with living there.'

'Oh, no,' cried the little hamster-woman. 'Oh, no, he couldn't be!'

'He is,' said Judy, 'and you won't help!' Stumblingly she began to get up.

'Won't you stay, dear, and hear about the Matterhorn?'

'No!' Judy tried to put her cup back on the dainty tea-table, but couldn't see properly for her tears. China fell, broke, as she turned from the table. She found the handle of the door and let herself out.

'Oh dear, oh dear, oh dear!' the little voice behind her was crying, but whether it was about the broken china or something else it was impossible to say.

Judy ran down the long passages and past the porter, who stared at her tear-wet face. When she got outside, she ran and ran, and then walked and walked. She knew she could have caught a bus home, but she didn't want to. She walked all the way, arriving nearly at dusk, to find her mother waiting anxiously for her. But, instead of questioning Judy at once, Mrs Cook drew her into the kitchen, where they were alone. Mike was in the sitting-room, watching a noisy television programme.

Mrs Cook said: 'Your dad telephoned from Walchester soon after you did. He said he wasn't feeling very well, so he's spending the night with your Aunt Edie.'

They stared at each other. Mr Cook detested his sister Edie. 'He'd do anything rather than come here,' said Judy. 'He's afraid.'

Mrs Cook nodded.

'Mum, we'll just have to move from here, for dad's sake.'

'I don't know that we can, Judy. Selling one house and buying another is very expensive; house-removal is expensive.'

'But if we stay here . . .'

Mrs Cook hesitated; then, 'Judy, what you were doing this afternoon – your calling on old Mrs Baxter – was it any use, any help?'

'No.'

Mrs Cook groaned aloud.

Judy's visit to Mrs Baxter had not led to the answering of any questions; but there was an outcome.

The next day, in the afternoon, Judy and Mike had come home from school and were in the kitchen with their mother. It was a gloomy tea. There was no doubt at all that their father would come home this time – after all, here were his wife and his children that he loved – but the homecoming seemed likely to be a grim and hopeless one.

From the kitchen they heard the click of the front gate. This was far too early to be Mr Cook himself, and, besides, there'd been no sound of a car. Mike, nearest to the window, looked out. 'No one we know,' he reported. 'An old lady.' He laughed to himself. 'She looks like a hamster.'

Judy was at the front door and opening it before Mrs Baxter had had time to ring. She brought her in and introduced her to the others, and Mrs Cook brewed fresh tea while the children made her comfortable in the sitting-room. Besides her handbag, Mrs Baxter was carrying a dumpy zip-up case which seemed heavy; she kept it by her. She was tired. 'Buses!' she murmured.

Mrs Cook brought her a cup of tea.

'Mrs Baxter doesn't take sugar, Mum,' said Judy.

They all sat round Mrs Baxter, trying not to stare at her, waiting for her to speak. She sipped her tea without looking at them.

'Your husband's not very well, I hear,' she said at last to Mrs Cook.

'No.'

'Not home from work yet'

'Not yet.'

Mrs Baxter was obviously relieved. She looked at them all now. 'And this is the rest of the family . . .' She smiled timidly at Mike: 'You're the baby of the family?'

Mike said, 'I'm younger than Judy. Mum, if it's OK, I think I'll go out on my bike with Charlie Feather.' He took something to eat and went.

Mrs Baxter said, 'We never had children.'

'A pity,' said Mrs Cook.

'Yes. Everything would be different, if it had been different.' Mrs Baxter paused. 'Do you know, I've never been back to this house – not even to the village – since Mr Baxter died?'

'It was very sad for you,' said Mrs Cook, not knowing what else to say.

'It's been a terrible *worry*,' said Mrs Baxter, as though sadness was not the thing that mattered. Again she paused. Judy could see that she was nerving herself to say something important. She had been brave and resolute to come all this way at all.

Mrs Cook could also see what Judy saw. 'You must be tired out,' she said

But Judy said gently: 'Why've you come?'

Mrs Baxter tried to speak, couldn't. Instead she opened the zip-up bag and dragged out of it a large, heavy book: *The Vegetable and Fruit Grower's Encyclopaedia and Vade-Mecum*. She pushed it into Mrs Cook's lap. 'It was Mr Baxter's,' she said. 'Give it to your husband. Tell him to use it and work hard in the garden, and I think things will right themselves in time. You need to humour him.'

Mrs Cook was bewildered. She seized upon the last remark: 'I humour him as much as I can, as it is. He's been so unwell.'

Mrs Baxter tittered. 'Good gracious, I didn't mean *your* husband: I meant mine. Humour Mr Baxter.'

'But – but he's dead and gone!'

Mrs Baxter's eyes filled with tears. 'That's just it: he isn't. Not both. He's dead, but not gone. He never meant to go. I knew what he intended; I knew the wickedness of it. I told him – I begged him on his deathbed; but he wouldn't listen. You know that bit of the burial service: "We brought nothing into this world, and it is certain that we can carry nothing out"? Well, there was something he'd dearly have liked to have taken out: he couldn't, so he stayed in this world with it: his garden. We were both good church-goers, but I believe he set his vegetable garden before his God. I know that he set it before me.' She wept afresh.

'Oh, dear, Mrs Baxter!' said Mrs Cook, much distressed.

'When he was dying,' said Mrs Baxter, after she had blown her nose, 'I could see there was something he wanted to say. I'd been reading the twenty-third Psalm to him – you know, about the Valley of the Shadow of Death. He was trying to speak. I leant right over him and he managed to whisper his very last words. He said, "Are the runner beans up yet?" Then he died.'

Nobody spoke. Mrs Baxter recovered herself and went on.

'I knew – I *knew* he wouldn't leave that garden, after he'd died. I just hoped the next owners would look after it as lovingly as he'd done, and then in time he'd be content to go. That's what I hoped and prayed. But the first lot of people were going to cover it with dog-kennels, and I heard that the second lot were going to lay it out with artificial streams and weeping willows and things. Well, he made their lives a misery, and they left. And now your husband . . .'

'He's just never liked gardening,' said Mrs Cook.

The two women stared at each other bleakly.

'Why can't Dad be allowed to watch telly?' asked Judy. Then, answering herself: 'Oh, I see: he ought to be working in the garden every spare minute in daylight and fine weather.'

'Mr Baxter quite enjoyed some of the gardening programmes, sometimes,' Mrs Baxter said defensively.

There was a long silence.

'It's lovely soil,' said Mrs Baxter persuasively. 'Easy to

work. Grows anything. That's why we came to live here, really. All my married life, I never had to buy a single vegetable. Fruit, too – raspberries, strawberries, gooseberries, all colours of currants. So much of everything, for just the two of us, that we had to give a lot of stuff away. We didn't grow plums or pears or apples – except for the Bramleys – because Mr Baxter wouldn't have trees shading the garden. But all those vegetables – you'd find it a great saving, with a family.'

'It seems hard on my husband,' said Mrs Cook.

'It's hard on mine,' said Mrs Baxter. 'Look at him!' Startled Mrs Cook and Judy looked where Mrs Baxter was looking, through the french windows and down the length of the garden. The sun fell on the weedy earth of the garden; on nothing else.

Mrs Cook turned her gaze back into the room, but Judy went on looking, staring until her eyes blurred and her vision was fogged with a kind of brown fogginess that was in the garden. Then suddenly she was afraid.

'But *look*!' said Mrs Baxter, and took Judy's hand in her own little paw that had grown soft and smooth from leisure in Senior House: '*Look!*' Judy looked where she pointed, and the brown fogginess seemed to concentrate itself and shape itself, and there dimly was the shape of an old man dressed in brown from his brown boots to his battered brown hat, with a piece of string tied round the middle of the old brown waterproof he was wearing. He stood in an attitude of dejection at the bottom of the garden, looking at the weeds.

Then Mrs Baxter let go of Judy's hand, and Judy saw him no more.

'That was his garden mac,' said Mrs Baxter. 'He would

wear it. When all the buttonholes had gone, as well as the buttons, and I wouldn't repair it any more, then he belted it on with string.'

'He looked so miserable,' said Judy. She had been feeling sorry for her father; now she began to feel sorry for Mr Baxter.

'Yes,' said Mrs Baxter. 'He'd like to go, I've no doubt of it; but he can't leave the garden in that state.' She sighed. She gathered up her handbag and the other empty bag.

'Don't go!' cried Mrs Cook and Judy together.

'What more can I do? I've told you; I've advised you. For *his* sake, too, I've begged you. No, I can't do more.'

She would not stay. She waddled out of the house and down the front path, and at the front gate met Mr Cook. He had just got out of the car. She gave him a scared little bob of a 'good-day', and scuttled past him and away.

Mr Cook came in wearily; his face was greyish. 'Who was that old dear?' he asked. But he did not really want to know.

His wife said to him, 'Arthur, Judy is going to get your tea – Won't you, love? – while I explain a lot of things. Come and sit down and listen.'

Mrs Cook talked and Mr Cook listened, and gradually his face began to change: something lifted from it, leaving it clear, almost happy, for the first time for many weeks. He was still listening when Judy brought his tea. At the end of Mrs Cook's explanation, Judy added hers: she told her father what – *whom* – she had seen in the garden, when Mrs Baxter had held her hand. Mr Cook began to laugh. 'You saw him, Judy? An old man all in brown with a piece of string tied round his middle – oh, Judy, my girl! When I began really seeing him, only the other day, I was sure I was going off my rocker! I was scared! I thought I was seeing things that no one else could see – things that weren't there at all! And you've seen him too, and he's just old man Baxter!' And Mr Cook laughed so much that he cried, and in the end he put his head down among the tea-things and sobbed and sobbed.

It was going to be all right, after all.

In Mr Baxter's old-fashioned mind, the man of the family was the one to do all the gardening. That was why, in what Judy considered a very unfair way, he had made a dead set at her father. But now all Mr Cook's family rallied to him. Even Mike, when the need was explained, left his bicycle for a while. They all helped in the garden. They dug and weeded and made bonfires of the worst weeds and began to build a compost heap of harmless garden rubbish. They planted seeds if it were not too late in the season, and bought plants when it was. Mr Cook followed the advice of the *Encyclopaedia*, and occasionally had excellent ideas of his own. When Judy asked him where he got them, he looked puzzled at himself and said he did not know. But she could guess.

Every spare moment that was daylight and fine, Mr Cook worked in the garden; and his illness was cured. His appetite came back; he slept like a top; and he would have enjoyed television again except that, in the middle of pro-grammes, he so often fell asleep from healthy exhaustion.

Well over a year later, on a holiday jaunt in Walchester, Judy was passing one of the cinemas. An audience mainly of Senior Citizens was coming out from an afternoon show-ing of *Deadly Amazon*. Judy felt a touch on her arm, soft yet insistent, like the voice that spoke, Mrs Baxter's: 'My dear, how – how is he?'

'Oh, Mrs Baxter, he's much, much better! Oh, thank you! He's really all right. My mum says my dad's as well as she's ever known him.'

'No, dear, I didn't mean your father. How is *he* – Mr Baxter?'

Judy said, 'We think he's gone. Dad hasn't seen the foggiest wisp of him for months; and Dad says it doesn't *feel* as if he's there any more. You see, Dad's got the garden going wonderfully now. We've had early potatoes and beans and peas – oh, and raspberries – and Dad plans to grow asparagus –'

'Ah,' said Mrs Baxter. 'No wonder Mr Baxter's gone. Gone off pleased, no doubt. That *is* nice. I don't think you need worry about his coming back. He has enough sense not to. It won't be long before your father can safely give up gardening, if he likes.'

'I'll tell him what you say,' Judy said doubtfully.

But, of course, it was too late. Once a gardener, always a gardener. 'I'll never give up now,' Mr Cook said. 'I'll be a gardener until my dying day.'

'But not after that, Arthur,' said his wife. 'Please.'

Other Puffins by Philippa Pearce

TOM'S MIDNIGHT GARDEN

Tom knew he was going to be bored and lonely in his uncle and aunt's home near the fens. And at first he was: until he made the strange and wonderful discovery that was too fantastic for anyone else to believe. A brilliantly original, unforgettable story.

WHAT THE NEIGHBOURS DID AND OTHER STORIES

Eight beautifully told stories of blackberrying, a boy's stolen outing with his grandfather, and the tree the boys never *meant* to cut down.

A DOG SO SMALL

Ben longs for a dog so much that he conjures one up out of his imagination.

MINNOW ON THE SAY

'You rotten thief!' shouted Adam, 'That's my canoe!' Not a hopeful start for a friendship, you might think, but David and Adam did become friends and were inseparable for the whole of that summer. A summer made unforgettable with the Minnow, the river Say, their treasure hunt and the awareness that their special friendship might soon be interrupted.

THE BATTLE OF BUBBLE AND SQUEAK

Sid and Peggy adore the two gerbils, Bubble and Squeak, but their mother detests them. A dingdong family battle results, and it's very uncertain which side has the most ammunition. Winner of the Whitbread Award.

THE ELM STREET LOT

The gang of children who meet on Elm Street are always in on the action, whether it's tracking down a lost hamster or going on safari across the roof tops.

THE WAY TO SATTIN SHORE

There is a mystery about Kate's family, but her family either knows nothing or will tell nothing. Her two elder brothers, her grandmother, her new friend Anna and her missing father all have a part to play in Kate's search to fit the jigsaw pieces of past and present to find a new picture for the future.

DANNY THE CHAMPION OF THE WORLD
Roald Dahl

Danny's playroom was the workshop of his father's filling station, his first toys were the greasy cogs and springs and pistons that filled it. By the time he was seven he could take a small engine to pieces and put it together again – pistons and crankshaft and all. So being eight was a lot of fun.

As it turned out, the year he was nine was even more exciting, for Danny's father had a deep, dark secret, he had kept hidden all Danny's life up till then, and soon after he'd revealed it Danny found himself engaged on a wild and difficult scheme.

A wildly funny, wickedly inventive romp of a book, suitable for every age.

UNDER THE MOUNTAIN
Maurice Gee

Rachel and Theo are twins. Apart from having red hair, there is nothing remarkable about them – or so they think. Imagine their horror, then, when they discover that only they can save the world from dominance by strange, powerful creatures who are waking, beneath the extinct volcanoes that surround the city, from a spell-bound sleep of thousands of years . . .

END OF TERM
Antonia Forest

For Lawrie Marlow, the best actress in the school, wanting to play the Shepherd Boy, the end of term play was the most important event of the term. Her twin, Nicola, though, had several other problems. She'd brought her hawk, Sprog, back with her, and this brought friendship with Esther Frewin, a shy new girl who had pet problems too. Then there was the grudge that Lois Sanger, the new games captain, seemed to have against her – just why *wasn't* she in the junior Netball team? And Nicky too was involved in the Christmas play – a momentous finish to the Marlow twins' first term in Lower IV A.

THE PEPPERMINT PIG
Nina Bawden

'You can't keep a pig indoors, Mother!' said Lily, quite scandalised. But Mother said, 'Give a pig a chance to keep clean and he'll take it,' and she gave the milk man a shilling for the little runt of a peppermint pig. Sure enough the little pig was happy, trotting busily round after Mother or toasting himself by the fire. He was clever too, and soon learned to be clean, and to answer to his name, which was Johnnie.

Everyone was happier because of the pig. He made Mother laugh. He comforted Theo, who was also too small for his age and as for Poll – the youngest – she counted the hours at school until she could get back home to dear, funny Johnnie. Somehow when she looked back on that eventful year in the country, though plenty of bad things had happened, what she really remembered was the things to do with Johnnie, who somehow kept the whole family united however bad things sometimes seemed.

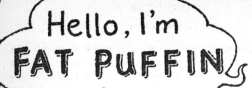